FLSF

OW00941578

GLADIATRIX

Also in this trilogy...

Victoria
Victrix

GLADIATRIX

FRANCES HENDRY

Hodder
Children's
Books

A division of Hodder Headline Limited

From the author

I've invented only the characters of Victoria and her Amazon friends and servants. Julia Felix's house in Pompeii can still be visited; Caenis, Sabinus, Domitian, Acte and the Emperors themselves are as true to actuality as I can make them, given the small amount of evidence actually available; and all the details about events in the Year of the Four Emperors, as it was known even then, are correct as far as I can discover them. Apart from the last dinner of Vitellius, the downfall and death of Nero and the other Emperors are as they really happened, according to the reports available, though I've sometimes inserted Victoria and her friends instead of the people we are told were actually there. In especial, Nero's incredible actions, orders and threats to the Senate are all as they were reported – though of course after his death, by his enemies.

Romans of importance usually had a given name or names, then the name of their family, then of a branch within the main tribe, e.g. Titus Flavius Vespasianus – the man named Titus, of the Flavian family, and the Vespasian branch (his mother's; his older brother carried on the father's name, Sabinus). They could also add extra names to celebrate some particular action or characteristic, or other members of the family, or adoptive parents, which sometimes led to very long names, e.g. Tiberius Claudius Drusus Nero Germanicus Britannicus – the Emperor Claudius. A freed slave took the name of his or her former owner, e.g. Antonia Caenis – Caenis, the freedwoman of Antonia. Victoria should actually be formally known as Glaevia Victoria Aegypta – Victoria, daughter of Aegyptus, former slave of Glaevius.

It was polite to call a person by the sub-family name, e.g. Vespasianus, or the family and last names, e.g. Julia Felix; only close friends would use the personal name of Titus or Julia. In fact, Julia Felix probably had another forename which has not been recorded, e.g. Portia Julia Felix, making 'Julia' her family name, one of the ancient Julian family, like Gaius Julius Caesar. However, for simplicity's sake I've stuck with what little we know about her from the villa where her mosaic portrait as a young woman adorned a wall.

The early 60s CE was a time of terrible brutality and decadence in Rome. Anyone who annoyed the Emperor, often merely by being too rich or too popular, could at any time receive a letter telling him to kill himself. If he refused, he would be charged with treason and executed anyway, after a show trial with paid witnesses and forged documents, and everything he owned would be confiscated so that his family was ruined. If he did kill himself, he could at least die with honour and only a quarter of his wealth would go to the Emperor. To survive took cleverness, the ability to toady charmingly to your superiors, and a lot of luck; to try to change society, as Victoria and her friend Caenis did, took a special kind of lunacy.

I hope you enjoy reading about Victoria as much as I have enjoyed writing about her and her gladiatorial exploits.

Frances Mary Hendry

I

He was aiming at the horses! Hissing in fury, Victoria hauled on the reins and fought for balance as her tiny chariot skidded round in a tight juddering swerve. Sprayed with gravel and sand thrown up right over the barrier, the legionaries and their families, almost twenty thousand people, yelled in excitement. Instead of in the chest, the Roman's javelin struck low in the front of Thunder's right haunch. The pony screamed and bucked, jerking the chariot and almost throwing Victoria out. The wooden spear-shaft dropped off as it was designed to do, but the iron head with its tang as long as Victoria's forearm stuck, half crippling the pony.

Even while he agreed before the combat that the horses were not to be harmed, the legionary charioteer, short and pugnacious, had been sneering. Many conservative people — and the legions were definitely traditional-minded — were disgusted by women in the arena at all, especially if they fought seriously against men, rather than in comedy bouts with dwarves or other women. Besides, a lot of Romans thought that you didn't need to keep your word to either a barbarian or a woman. He — and they — would learn that that didn't pay!

* * *

The Fifth, Twelfth and Third Legions were garrisoned near Antioch, the third biggest city in the Empire, to fight the constant rebellions at the eastern end of the Mare Nostra. The evening before, they had laid on a lavish party for the Amazons' touring troupe of gladiatrixes and their opponents; the traditional last dinner before games in which a gladiator might well die.

Victoria always took a sardonic pleasure in the awkwardness people had in dealing with her. Romans, even slaves, saw ordinary gladiators as scum, and gladiatrixes as worse, but she was special; a rich champion, a celebrity all over the world, and a favourite of Emperor Nero himself. The hard-bitten centurions, career soldiers risen from the ranks, most in their second fifteen-year enlistment, would have welcomed her with bawdy gusto, as they did her comrades of the Amazons. Most of the young officers were noblemen serving three or four years with the army as a first step on the career path which they hoped would lead them to a consulship. They would be raffishly intrigued. But she'd never fit on the top couches with the legion commanders, the legates and their snobbish wives.

This lot had handled it quite well. The feast was set out on a wide ring of trestle tables on the parade ground, where next day an arena would be laid out with a wooden barrier and tiered benches, and the packed sandy gravel would be stained with blood. The senior officers, the three legates and their tribunes, were in small groups of couches dotted round the circle of carpet-draped benches for almost two hundred centurions, their wives and guests. She was ushered round by a snooty young junior tribune, to pause, perch, eat and chat as she went.

Handy. No-one would realise what she was doing. Bored garrison officers would talk about her for months, she knew, so she chatted gently, spreading hints and scandal wherever she stopped, for them to discuss and develop in their own time.

Here – 'Yes, my tattoos are British.' She proudly smoothed the vivid patterns swirling over her scarred, hairless scalp. 'Striking, eh? My father was a centurion there under Vespasian. Excellent officer, he said. But my mother was British, that's why I have these, and this torc.' She touched the ring of twisted gold round her neck. 'I nearly died in the burning of Londinium during Boudicca's rebellion, and the tribes killed my family.' That was true, if not all the truth, and well known; and it established her on Rome's side.

No-one here knew of her vivid memories of Queen Boudicca back in Britain, who had whispered as she died, 'Destroy Rome. I lay it on you, a command from the gods. Destroy Rome . . .' No-one would realise what Victoria was trying to do, not until she succeeded.

If she succeeded. If Bouda favoured her . . .

She moved on to the next group – 'Where have we toured? You name it, we've been there!'

Her second-in-command, the retiarius Africa, being lavishly entertained by the Third's centurions, added details. 'North to Germania, both Gauls, south through Hispania, Lusitania, east all along the coast of Africa from Morocco to Egypt. Alexandria loved us!' Her wide grin bright against her dark skin, she shimmied in triumph, sending the tiny bells on her deep-yellow fringes into a tinkling frenzy, to whistles and deep growls of approval. 'Then we sailed here, north past Judaea. No, we didn't stop there. Gladiators don't like wars. Bad for business – people who are fighting don't want to pay to watch us do it!'

'The trouble there is far worse, isn't it, since Corbulo died?' Victoria asked innocently. Nero had ordered General Corbulo to commit suicide; she knew how much they had respected him. 'Finest general in the empire, I heard! A cursed shame!' They growled agreement. 'But the Emperor is jealous of noble, popular people, especially generals. And scared. He thinks they're a threat, could rebel. Might be right! Nobody's safe nowadays!' This last comment could be taken more ways than one. Some laughed; others scowled; good.

Don't lose sight of the main point. 'But General Vespasian seems to be doing well. His troops think he's the best since Romulus. We're off to Ephesus next, and then to Moesia, up on the Danube north of Greece. You're heading that way soon, aren't you? We'll maybe travel up with you. So you can see more of Africa here!' She grinned down at the tall black girl, gorgeous, exotic and always popular, chuckled at the soldiers' enthusiastic whistles and comments, and moved on.

To the next group – 'Yes, the Domus Aurea is finished. Tinsel Towers, they call it, or ruder things that I'm too ladylike to mention in polite company!' They roared with laughter, and added some of the other names for the palace. 'Yes, you've heard about it. You'd not believe how enormous! Covers half of Rome. Most of what he burnt – sorry, what those Jews burnt!' Everybody thought that Nero himself had set the blaze to clear space for his new home. She knew he hadn't started it – not the first day, anyway. But the belief was very useful.

'He's levied hefty fire taxes to pay for the rebuilding – doesn't make him popular! Emptied the treasury, desperate for money. Tells his judges, "You know what I want!" So everybody's found guilty, and fines are crippling. Did you hear, he sent out a freedman to sell some of his royal purple dye in the market – you know, the one only *he's* allowed to use? And when a stupid woman bought and used it, he prosecuted her, guilty of course, confiscated everything she had, left her family flat-broke and had her stripped there and then, left her naked in the court.' Her audience laughed, but sourly. 'He even spent on his new little cottage all the money that should have bought the grain for the free rations for the city; the Praetorians have been busy as bees in a beanfield putting down food riots. Nero says, "Now at last I can live like a human being!" What does he think the rest of us are, eh?' The laughter was even sourer.

'Oh – and I hear Rome's to be renamed. Guess what? Neropolis.' Shrugging, smiling, she left disgusted snarls behind her and moved on.

At her next stop – 'He's just gone home, after his jaunt through Greece to take part in all their little games.' This group sneered. Actors and public entertainers were almost as despised as gladiators; for an emperor to perform in public was disgusting, degraded all Romans. She looked snootily at them, imitating the Emperor – risky, but worth it. ' "The Greeks alone are worthy of my efforts!" ' Romans looked down on Greeks; their faces stiffened. 'He took five thousand paid applauders with him. And had all the dates moved to fit his trip, even the Olympics. Won every wreath for singing and poetry. Two thousand, I hear. Well, who'd dare vote against him?'

'And all the prizes for chariot driving.' The primus pilus, second in authority only to the legate himself, sniffed in contempt. 'Even for the Olympic ten-horse race, though he fell out and never finished.' Someone actually spat.

Further round, the legate of the Twelfth was discussing the rebellion in Judaea. 'Need to sort out these revolting people!' Everybody laughed, rather to his surprise. 'Eh? Oh – a joke, yes . . . But the new governor, General Vespasian, seems competent.'

Handy that he brought it up himself. 'My father fought under Vespasian, said he was exceptionally good. You know why he was sent here?' Victoria asked. 'The real story?'

The officers looked intrigued. 'Useful reputation, but a provincial nobody, no famous ancestors, no political clout. No threat,' the legate suggested.

'Not like Corbulo, no. Right. But Nero took Vespasian among his courtiers on his tour of Greece. Now, you know anybody caught leaving one of Nero's performances can be executed.'

'People pretend to be ill, or even to die, to get away,' someone commented.

'Or have babies! Yes, one woman actually did! Bad timing – or good, eh? Well, Vespasian fell asleep during a performance. Tactless! Had to run for his life!' The soldiers guffawed. Victoria chortled with them. 'So I think Nero sent him here to punish him, hoping he'd fail. Never mind what happens to the poor soldiers, eh? But maybe I'm wrong, or maybe the Emperor is. Maybe he sent the right man. Vespasian isn't the failing kind.'

The senior tribune pursed his lips. 'Have you heard? An ox ploughing in a field near Vespasian's house broke away and fell to its knees before him!'

Though she knew the story, Victoria gasped as if awed. 'That's an omen of imperial power, isn't it? Whoo! I've heard of others, too, but he keeps them quiet, it's dangerous to talk about them. And last month, lightning wrecked the statues of the Emperors in the Temple of the Caesars. Not a good sign for Nero, eh?' Someone whistled in wonder. Superstitious lot, these Romans! She put a finger to her lips. 'Ssh!' Another seed for thought . . .

Most of the tribunes, sons of senators or equites who had heard political talk all their lives, appreciated her scandalous backstairs stories about the greedy, incompetent palace hangers-on; no those who actually ran the Empire while Nero was swanning round enjoying himself. 'Who else could do it, then?' she asked casually after a while. 'Governor Mucianus in Syria here? Couldn't run a booze-up in a brewery? Oh, Mars! Who, then? An army man, trained and experienced?'

They dismissed several governors, ex-consuls and generals with slanderous tales of their ineptitude or corruption, till someone eventually mentioned Vespasian. 'Now there's a real possibility,' she observed. 'My father served under him in the invasion of Britain, said he was honest, hard-working, efficient – the best officer he ever knew. His older brother Sabinus is Rome's Urban Prefect, running the place so well they won't let him retire. His older son Titus is in Judaea with him, and did well in Germania and Britain, I'm told. The younger one, Domitian, is about seventeen. At least there would be an heir. After Nero, who is there? He's murdered all – oops, can't say that! I mean there's none of the imperial family left. Even his stepson, Poppaea's boy – you know, the empress he kicked to death – oh, can't say that either, even if I was there when he

8

did it. The Empress who died. The lad was playing emperor with his pals in the garden. Treason! Off to the strangler! Nine years old.' The officers looked disgusted, not surprised.

'The last of the Caesar family was Antonia, the sister of Nero's first wife, Octavia – you remember, the one he accused of treason and had executed?' They remembered; it had been a shocking scandal. 'He wanted Antonia to marry him – after killing her sister! She refused, so he accused her of treason too. Goodbye, Antonia!' Someone spat. Victoria shrugged. 'He's married someone else now – can't remember her name, she keeps out of sight as far as she can, sensible woman. But no children. Scarcely surprising, considering the Emperor's Greek habits. You've heard he's mad about a pretty slave boy? Sporus, the image of Poppaea, I'm told. Nero had him made a eunuch and dresses him like her; they say he's even gone through a marriage ceremony with the lad.' Jaws dropped and lips tightened. Enough spice in that pudding . . . 'So the Senate would have to pick somebody – or more likely the army, like when the Praetorians killed Caligula and made old Claudius Emperor.' Another seed . . .

Then an interruption. A man came running. 'Victrix, imperial messenger just arrived. Letter for you from the Emperor!'

The Twelfth's officers were all agog, ears flapping. A personal letter from Nero!

Victoria controlled the hippopotamuses suddenly

stampeding through her stomach, broke the seal and read it herself, rather to their surprise – despite her reputation they hadn't expected her to be able to read. 'His Imperial Majesty summons me to Rome.' Why? What would she meet there? A welcome? Or a curt note telling her to commit suicide? If anyone had realised what she was really doing . . . 'Where's Africa – oh, there you are, plum. You heard – of course you did, you're always ahead of the news. Will you lead the Amazons on to Ephesus and Moesia? We've got contracts there for six shows.'

Africa, always reliable, nodded. 'You don't want us to come with you?'

It would make her feel safer, but falsely; they'd just be drawn into any trouble she might be in. Better if they stayed clear. 'No, mustn't let down our fans up north. Sorry to lay all the organising on you, but I'll go back alone.' She glanced round at her audience. 'But not until after tomorrow's games! I'll not let you down either!' The officers cheered her.

'The Emperor's command is official business, and I've letters to send back,' the legate declared. 'We'll arrange an army escort and a ship for you.'

'Thank you, sir! That will make my trip far easier and quicker.'

He beamed. 'In return, can I propose an extra event? We'd like to see a real chariot contest – I have a charioteer . . .'

As leader and champion of the Amazons, and after his generous offer of help, she could scarcely refuse.

Now, though, she was in trouble.

Victoria was tired, in her third combat today. This morning, after some beast hunts and a show of drill by a crack team from the Twelfth Legion, she and the other Amazons had put on a skilful display of fancy driving and spear-throwing, and showy rehearsed fights – dangerous but not deadly. During the noon rest, executions of criminals entertained the crowd, one witch being torn by hyenas, which Victoria had thought was nastily messy even for the legions.

Then, in the main part of the show, the twenty Amazons had faced some challengers from the legions and several local Syrian gladiators. One of her girls had been killed and eleven wounded, six of whom were beaten but spared by the crowd. Victoria herself had had a hard fight against a powerful Abyssinian secutor, bigger and stronger than she was, but not as fast in his heavy armour nor as ring-wise; when he stabbed deep into her thigh, scraping the bone, he hadn't withdrawn his sword fast enough to stop her killing him. In the exhilaration of combat she had barely noticed the wound, but now it was sickeningly painful, which didn't matter, and weakened, which did.

And now this chariot fight. Her opponent couldn't afford to lose; if she won, but he survived, his officers and comrades would make his life a misery. So she knew his plan; this

11

non-accidental accident to cripple her horses, and apologies to her corpse . . . Curse him! Without her horses she was lost, he could circle round her and pick her off at leisure.

This might be her last fight . . .

No! Never give up!

Victoria set Thunder and Lightning to run round the ring away from the soldier. 'Go on, Thunder, brave soul! Bear up bravely for me!' Had she time? Maybe . . . The soldier's bigger, heavier horses were a touch clumsy and nervous in this smallish arena, and had been showered and spooked by the flying gravel of her swerve, and the crowd's roar. He was having some trouble getting them back under control.

She tied the reins and scrambled forward, out along the pole. Applause rolled round the arena as she jumped to straddle the hurt pony. Just as well it was Thunder who had been hurt, he was steadier than Lightning, less liable to panic. However, the small, sturdy pony was purely a driven beast, not accustomed to being ridden, and also in pain with every step. He shied, nearly throwing her under the wheels — she had never been a good rider. She clung like a leopard, leant down and jerked the javelin-head free. As Thunder flinched and screamed, she slithered back onto the pole, slipped, the crowd yelled, she grabbed Lightning's tail to shove herself up, scrabbled back, kneeling, and seized her reins again.

The Roman's next javelin was already in the air. The small

shield strapped to her left forearm just deflected the javelin-point, but the shaft banged her nose — curse this open driving helmet, you could see where you were going but it was little protection — Bouda, it hurt! She could barely see, blood splattering everywhere was it broken? — Never mind that, concentrate!

He still had two spears, to her last one. Was she certain of nailing him? No, he was armoured and half hidden by the chariot side. Aim at his horses, as he had at hers? Dishonourable. Think fast . . .

She scrambled to her feet, to throw better, and made a great show of fleeing. 'Go, Thunder, go, Lightning, go, my beauties!' The soldier yelled in triumph, galloping in pursuit round the arena, overtaking fast while his comrades cheered him on, curse them!

The leather floor of the chariot was suspended on strong straps from springy birch-root arches along the sides, which cushioned the worst of the jounces. The springs were just kneel-high, though, so unlike the Roman in his heavy, waist-high wooden chariot Victoria had nothing to hold onto. However, she had trained long and hard for this. Bent-kneed, ignoring the pain, she balanced and judged her moment to haul on the reins. 'Turn, turn, my doves, and whoa!' The little vehicle juddered round sideways, she threw her weight to the inside, to keep from overturning and avoid being tossed out, and the Roman's horses swerved wildly to pass, disturbing his aim. As he roared by, Victoria twisted and steadied herself to throw her last spear. He jeered as it flew far too low.

Then he recognised the trap and yelled in horrified anticipation.

Her spear slammed through his wheel to stick fast in the solid chariot body. His spokes smashed against the shaft, shattered and showered. His chariot tipped and crashed. Like a racing driver, he had tied the reins to his waist. Screaming, he was dragged along the gravel while his crippled chariot bounced over him round the ring.

The first-aid men raced out with a stretcher. Victoria smiled tightly in satisfaction. That would teach the stupid scumbag to keep his word!

'Victrix! Victrix! Victrix!' Though she had defeated and possibly killed their champion, the legions were cheering her. In the bedlam, she pulled off her helmet and drove a lap of honour, easing the hurt pony round. Her tattooed scalp and the blood on her face glowed in the sunshine.

Fiercely, she screamed her victory war-cry. No-one here would understand Iceni. Just as well. 'Death! Death to Rome!'

II

Late in May, tired after a long, stormy voyage, Victoria drew rein at the top of the path through the olive groves down to her small villa three miles east of Rome. Though she had lived here for only a short time after Nero had given it to her, it felt like coming home. Now for a hot bath, and a cup of cool wine on her terrace looking down over the orchard to the river . . .

But what had happened to it? The little four-roomed house looked like a slum. Several of its red tiles were missing. Greasy smoke belched from the window and door of the kitchen, built far enough away from the house to avoid danger of fire – obviously just as well. Every corner was silted up with rubbish. Weeds flourished everywhere, including the orchard and vineyard, though the vegetable garden showed signs of recent hoeing. The thatch of the small stable had been inexpertly patched with straw, bright yellow amid the brown. No hens nor geese, nor the white doves that used to preen on the roofs. A stink of burnt food and pigs; two small black ones were rootling round the doorway of the bathhouse – where was the door? Some washing draggled over a sagging fence. Several of her fruit trees had been cut down. Women's voices were screeching. Squatters.

The agency she had bought her steward Smarandax from had guaranteed that he was highly-trained and reliable. Oh, Vesta, she'd have to have words with him. And them.

Wearily, she called to the decurion of the small troop of cavalrymen who had escorted her from Antioch, 'We're here, Barius, but I've been invaded! It looks as if I might need you. Anyway, come in and get a drink, if there is anything, and a token of thanks for your help.' Pleased at the promise of some action and a tip, the riders trotted behind her chariot down the path.

Squealing, a scrawny girl of about twelve darted out of the front door, leapt the five shallow steps and shot across the drive right under the noses of the ponies. They shied violently, jolting the chariot sideways. Victoria fell out.

Three big boys waving dead rats raced shouting after the child, skidded to a halt, gawped at the arrivals and swerved rapidly away round a corner.

A smaller boy shot out of the door shrieking, 'Leave her alone, you pigs!' He gasped at the ponies, which were rearing, ready to bolt, and instantly raced forward between the flailing hooves to grab their bridles without flinching, calling, 'Quiet there, quiet!' though they jerked him off his feet.

The girl scurried back to the porch, yelling, 'Mum! Mum!'

'Who're you?' Victoria demanded, struggling to her feet. The cavalrymen were laughing, Bouda curse them!

Clutching the reins, swung about by the ponies like a flag on a windy day, the skinny lad still answered defiantly. 'Oppio,' he grunted. 'Settle down, you stupid big lummoxes! Quiet, now, quiet! I lives here.'

'Since when? Who said you could stay, you and the others there?' Victoria's leg hurt, she had hit her head, she was tired and mortified at falling out in front of the soldiers, and her temper was boiling.

'We was all burnt out in the big fire, lookin' for a place, an' there weren't nobody here 'cep' Smartypants.' Who? Oh, Smarandax, of course. The boy spoke without taking his attention off the calming ponies. 'Tried to get us out, he did, huh, couldn't chase a dormouse, Drusus an' his gang beat him up shockin'. But we ain't like them, we work, me an' Celia, in the garden, an' Mum cooks, an' we put out the stable roof when Drusus set it alight, an' mended it wi' straw. Drusus an' them, they don't do nowt, drop dirt at their backsides like their pigs, but—'

Behind him, a square, neat woman in her early thirties bustled out of the door, adjusting the scarf that tied back her black curls. 'Yes, all right, Celia, I'll see to it! Oppio! Come away from them horses this instant, you'll get yourself killed . . .' Her eyes flickered from Victoria's clothes to her scalp to her furious face. The woman shut her mouth convulsively, gulped, braced herself and came forward down the steps. 'Lady Victrix? Oh, Isis! Celia! Celia, come on, they won't eat you, run for

Smarandax, he's fishing, tell him his mistress is home. Lady, I'm Mira, we come here, me an' the kids – I can explain . . . the fire—'

'Oppio's your son? He did explain.' Victoria's bad leg wobbled under her.

Mira's arm was instantly under her shoulder. 'Just lean on me, dear. Oppio, tie them horses to a tree an' hold the door. For once do what you're told without arguing!'

Dizzy, reluctantly glad of the support, Victoria allowed herself to be helped towards the steps.

A minor mob of eight men, several boys, and a dozen women and girls suddenly rampaged out, all grubby and slovenly, shouting and waving knives, clubs or ladles.

Victoria whipped out her sword. Danger always gave her extra strength. Mira yipped and sensibly jumped back, out of the sword's reach but near enough to support Victoria if she staggered again.

'We ain't movin'!' the biggest man bellowed.

His supporters yelled agreement: 'Been here a year! An' more! Can't throw us out! We knows our rights!'

Mira protested, 'This is Victrix, the owner!'

'Scummy gladiatrixes, scabby hags! We're free men! We lives here! Ow!' The gang's shouts turned to yelps.

'Not no more you don't,' Barius declared cheerfully. At his gesture, the troopers had moved gently to surround the gang, and the spear-points had dropped and pricked. 'An' you got

18

no rights here neither. You're ratty squatters. An' you're leaving. Now.'

Smarandax was racing up the path, his beaky nose and thin face flushed with worry and excitement. 'Mistress, oh mistress, you're back, welcome, what a way to be greeted, these stinking ruffians, I'm sorry, the Praetorians wouldn't help get them out, nor the vigiles, nobody would, welcome home, sorry about, er, they've eaten all the poultry, and the pigeons, and burnt the bathhouse door, thieving mucky drunken thugs—'

Victoria raised a hand. 'Later, tell me later. Barius, get rid of them, will you?' She vaguely noticed Mira's appalled, urgent glance at her steward.

Biting his lip, Smarandax forced himself to speak up. 'Er, this woman, mistress, can she – er, yes, Mira, her name is, and her children, they're – I'm – we're – er . . .' Panting, blushing, bobbing his head nervously, the scrawny young man nodded towards Mira.

Natural, Victoria supposed. 'Right. Barius, they can stay, but the bullies . . .'

'We'll see 'em off for you, Victrix!' The cavalryman grinned down at the gang's outcry of curses and pleading. 'You grotty lumps of dogshit, an' all your runty mongrel brats, if you're still here when I count two hundred, you stay – to fertilise the roses!'

Smarandax was almost sobbing in triumph. A skinny, meagre

19

twenty-six, he'd not been forceful enough to keep the intruders out alone, force them to leave, nor convince the neighbours to help. He had suffered not just the squatters' fists and boots, but also agonies of humiliation at their contempt and the damage they had done to the house left in his care. Now he'd see the back of the hooligans!

'Thank you, lady! We'll have the place clean an' tidy in no time, we will, once that lot's gone.' Mira was briskly grateful. 'Now come in an' sit down – Celia, get the lady a drink o' my willow-bark cordial for her poor head, quick as you can, petal – an' I'll sort yer room, yes, they used it, lady, couldn't stop 'em, but two shakes of a lamb's tail, we'll have their mess cleared out an' make up the bed again fresh an' you can lie down, you're beat.'

'I'll see t'yer hosses, lady!' the boy assured her, and scowled as the troopers laughed.

With relief, Victoria decided she could leave them to organise everything, at least for the moment, and allowed herself to be helped in. Within five minutes she could lie down in semi-dark. 'Tell Smarandax twenty sesterces for the soldiers,' she muttered just before sleep stunned her.

When she woke next day the house was quiet. A fresh shirt and trousers were laid out for her, a basin of warm water and a rough cloth, a jug of well-watered wine under a damp cloth to cool it, fresh rolls, cheese and honeycomb. Much of her vigour restored after a wash and breakfast, she strolled out to the terrace, still chewing, to look round.

Smarandax, listening for movement, met her nervously. 'Good morning, mistress, I hope you slept well? Er, the cavalry, they've left, mistress, thanking you, yes, er, I took the money from your purse, I hope that was . . . Yes, thank you, lady. And Drusus and his friends won't dare come back, no, not when you're here yourself. Er, that Mira and her girl, they're good reliable workers, yes, and, er, good in the garden, though you'll never see young Celia, so shy. The little boy too, stubborn as a rock, but nippy and willing. They'll not ask much pay, no, not when you've been so kind, er, just their keep and, er, maybe a few asses?' His anxiety calmed slightly as she nodded. 'The others – oh, filthy mess they've left! But we're getting cleared away, oh, yes. And, er, they brought pigs with them, doing well in the woods down by the river, and the windfall fruit, they couldn't find them all, not with the soldiers chasing them off, no, so that's a small—'

'Tell me this evening,' Victoria interrupted. 'I'm summoned to court, Smarandax. Get out my best clothes—'

'They're unpacked and pressed all ready, mistress, and the water hot in the bathhouse.' The young steward had been bought not long before the Amazons left on tour. Having had little time to learn what his mistress was like, he was terrified of being punished for the damage done to the estate, and desperately eager to please.

21

Victoria patted his arm. 'Calm down, calm down! You couldn't beat that gang, not on your own. I'm glad you stayed at all, rather than running away as many would have done.'

She felt embarrassed by the depth of gratitude on his face.

Oppio had her ponies, freshly groomed, harnessed to the chariot by the time Victoria was dressed. She studied him; a skinny ten or eleven, not pretty – a front tooth missing and a bad cast in his right eye – but wiry, and his eyes were bright. 'Thank you.' She hopped up to kneel, took the reins and clicked her tongue to start forward. The little chariot bounced. The boy had jumped in to kneel behind her, arms spread to grip the side arches, his face blissful.

She drew up. 'Out.'

'But lady, you'll need somebody to hold 'em while you're wi' the Emperor.'

'You think there are no grooms at the Domus Aurea? In any case, wheeled vehicles are banned in Rome during the day, I'll have to leave them at a stable outside the walls. Out.'

'So you'll need somebody to see to 'em there! I can water 'em, have 'em ready for you when you comes back. Or if you drops summat, lady, you got a bad leg, you needs somebody to hop down an' get it for you. Or clear trees off the road—'

'Trees? You? Knee-high to a centipede?'

'I'm stronger 'n I looks. Lemme come, lady, I'll be useful.'

She glared; he didn't move. 'Smarandax said you were stubborn.'

He nodded, his smile nervously cocky. 'As a mule.'

'As ten mules, it looks like.' She suddenly grinned at the snip of a lad. 'You remind me of me, learning to fight though I knew my father would probably beat me . . . All right – but you've got to sit still and not jounce about.'

He simply nodded again, his face lighting up like a rainbow, and settled more solidly.

As she drove on up the path to the road, she was chuckling. 'You like horses? I saw you're not afraid of them. Would you like to learn to drive?'

'Oh, yes, lady! Yes! Gonna be a racin' driver, wi' the Blues, they're the best team. Couldn't leave Mum an' Celia, not wi' Dad dyin' in the big fire, but I'll do it yet, by Castor an' Pollux I will.'

She might have caused his father's death. She felt – responsible. Besides, his chirpy determination amused her. 'I'd not bet against you. Ever worked with horses?'

'On'y donkeys, lady. But I'll learn!'

He did, too. By the time they reached the Viminal Gate into Rome, beside the Praetorian barracks, he had persuaded her to let him kneel in front of her, holding the reins beyond her hands to get the feel of the ponies' mouths, already doing more actual driving than she had expected. She stopped before

23

the gate. 'Take them over to that stable – no, lead them, don't try to drive them alone yet!'

Oppio grinned up at her. 'Yes, lady. We'll be ready for you when you comes out.'

She hoped she did . . . 'Good man.' He beamed after her as she headed for the wide gateway in the city wall.

Rome itself was drastically changed. Outside the city walls new suburbs were spreading like weeds. Since she had seen the magnificence of Egypt, the city inside the walls felt surprisingly small and cramped now. Its temples, even the great gilded one to Jupiter on the Capitoline Hill above the Forum, were less imposing than she remembered. However, the rebuilt streets of stone and multicoloured stucco houses were wider, better paved, more elegant and safer from fire than the old higgledy vennels of high, plastered-wood tenements. Victoria approved.

She approved less of the vast Domus Aurea, sprawling marble mosaics and gold tiles across its hillside. Glitter City; Castle Swanky. Breathtaking, yes; but several thousand people had lived there.

To her surprise and pleasure, many people greeted her, 'Victrix! Welcome home!' She was memorable, of course, a handspan taller than most Roman men, with tattooed head, brilliant Iceni checked and striped trousers and shirt, her famous wolfskin jerkin with the head snarling between her shoulders, and her sword, a gift from Nero. Not her own old sword, Needle, the treasured gift from her uncle in Britain that had been lost during the great fire, but a good, well-balanced blade from the best swordsmith in Capua.

It caused problems with the Praetorians. They resented her extraordinary privilege of carrying weapons in public, and the decurion guarding the gate in the palace wall refused to let her pass with it. Using the controlled assertiveness she had learnt over the past months, instead of hitting him or kicking the gate open she merely sneered down at him. 'The Emperor himself gave me permission to carry it even in his presence. You really want to explain to Nero that you disagree with his judgement?' Sourly he compromised, motioning to his men to open the gate just enough to let her squeeze in. Stupid pig.

Under high-piled, threatening clouds she limped across the beautiful park that replaced half of the old Rome, an artificial small-scale landscape of farmland, vineyards and fruit-tree groves where Nero could stroll, maybe with his bow, shooting birds specially released for him. Other game, hares and dainty gazelles – nothing dangerous like boar or wolves, she noted sardonically – grazed among statues, rose-beds and fountains in front of offices, slave quarters, summerhouses, built to look like a miniature city. Peacocks mewed and posed under a colonnade a mile long bordering a wide lake, where little rainbow gondolas bobbed at gaily-striped poles.

The main entrance was tall enough to admit two elephants piggy-back. On a pillar taller than twenty men before it towered the Colossus, a golden statue of Nero with the lyre and sun-ray headdress of Apollo – an insult to the god, to claim to be like him! The statue was triple life-size – which was legally forbidden, as blasphemous arrogance – and made, Victoria knew, of statues stolen from Rome's temples and melted down. Threefold sacrilege; Nero would pay for it, if the Roman gods had any power.

Meantime, she'd go head high to face whatever the Emperor had in mind for her. Her friend Petronius, the ultimate courtier, would have advised her what to expect, but last year Nero had ordered him to kill himself. Her teeth clenched; it might be her turn today.

'Miss Victrix! How pleasant to see you again!' The stewards' smiles seemed genuine, a good sign – they always knew who was in or out of favour. 'I'll show you the way – it's a maze!' True; and an opulent one. The interlacing passages and halls were glittering with gold, crowded with statues, floored with marbles from all over the Empire, walled and roofed with intricate ivory and ebony fretwork, exquisite painted frescoes, or mosaics made of semi-precious stones. The ceilings were so high, their painted clouds might almost have drifted in from outside. It was a staggering display of wealth and power.

Suddenly she saw a friend; Acte, the slave who was perhaps the only person who truly loved Nero, the only person he cared for, the woman he had actually wanted to marry once.

Even with this Sporus boy in the palace, and Nero's new wife
– what was her name? – sweet, gentle, simple Acte would still
be devotedly looking after her master. Victoria stuck two
fingers in her mouth and whistled. Vulgar, but effective. She
chuckled as all within earshot jumped like startled cats.

Acte hurried towards her, smiling a welcome. 'Victrix! I
mean Victoria. How nice! How are you? Oh, you're limping.
What's wrong? Have you hurt yourself?'

Victoria fought down the temptation to say, 'No, I always
walk this way,' or 'It's woodworm.' Teasing Acte wasn't fair. 'A
stab in my leg, Acte dear. You look well. How is Nero today?
What's he doing?'

Acte hesitated. Two questions at a time was a lot for her to
handle. 'He's well. He's playing the water-organ.' What was
that? 'But he's terribly worried.'

'About the new rebellion in Germania?' Victoria asked. 'I
was hearing about it.'

Acte blinked. 'Well, er, no, not that . . . He's lost his sacred
Isis figurine that protects him. We can't find it anywhere! So
upsetting! Though he doesn't show it, he's so brave.'

That was not a word Victoria herself had ever applied to
Nero. Reckless, careless, impulsive, yes; brave, no. But she
mustn't hang about. Especially since, having lost his talisman,
Nero might not look on her with as much favour as before.
Just as he had first welcomed her because she looked like it,
now he might even dispose of her, blaming her somehow for

27

the loss of the little idol, or simply to make her death match its disappearance. Oh, Bouda protect her! 'Nero summoned me.'

'Yes, yes of course, you must go to him at once, I understand. We can talk later.' Acte waved, looking rather lonely, as Victoria limped off behind her patient guide.

Hideous moanings were echoing down the passageways. What on earth . . .?

On a low dais in the centre of an octagonal hall, the Emperor stood pulling and pushing small levers on a gilded box of pipes which shook and shivered. Two slaves pumped larger levers behind it. Nero's fair beard and outrageously theatrical curls, and the armpits of his gold-trimmed crimson tunic, were damp with sweat. He had grown quite podgy.

Unexpectedly, Victoria's throat and belly tightened with loathing at the sight of him.

Hide it! Control!

The din died. Nero bowed his head modestly to the cheering of his clients, the toadies and self-seeking senators who formed his court. 'Enchanting! Sublime! What skill! Such exquisite phrasing! A masterpiece, Caesar! As ever!' Everyone ignored a sudden resonating burp from the apparatus.

A delicate young woman was sitting on the nearest couch, superbly jewelled, very feminine in the frilly style that Nero liked. In dramatic ecstasy, she sighed melodiously, 'Oh, darling, how heart-stoppingly splendid!'

'The merest trifle, Sporus!' Nero protested modestly. Two

28

pretty children patted his face and hands with hot, damp towels, careful not to damage his make-up, while he sank onto the embroidered cushions beside Sporus, kissed the youth – Victoria could feel revulsion radiating from several older, more conservative senators – and opened his mouth like a baby to accept spoonfuls of whipped cream mixed with fruit juice and snow, from a pearl-encrusted cup. 'Ah, delicious, my dear! But you are so naughty, all of you! You flatter me!'

'No, no, never!' echoed through the hall. 'We know you despise flattery, Caesar!'

As he agreed, flattered, Nero's eyes rose to Victoria behind them.

Now for it; welcome – or death.

Nero clapped his hands in extravagant joy. 'Victrix! My Imperial Gladiatrix! At last!'

A passage opened through the crowd of nobles, allowing her to stride forward hiding her limp and her relief, draw her sword and salute flamboyantly. 'Hail, Caesar!'

No questions about how she was, had she had a good journey; as always, Nero was totally self-absorbed. Fortunately, no mention of the little idol either. He beamed round at the assembly. 'Gentlemen, Victrix is always absolutely frank. Let us hear her opinion of my new water-organ.' He gestured proudly to the box. 'The latest invention!'

'And you are its finest player, Caesar!' someone called.

'Too kind!' All demure, 'So, Victrix, what did you think of it? Honestly, now!'

She was an uncivilised barbarian; amuse him, and she could tell the truth. 'I thought it sounded like a cow with toothache.' Jaws dropped all round, including Nero's. Had she gone too far? 'Haunting, I admit. Uncanny. Once I'm used to it, Caesar, I may appreciate it more. But I prefer your singing.'

No need to say how little she liked that, either.

For several seconds there was a frozen silence, while Nero considered her comment. Then he clapped his hands again, glowing. 'Splendid integrity! Yes indeed, it is strange, eerie. Your British bards appreciate it – one was sent to me recently, he was astounded, astounded!' Victoria controlled her eyebrows; what a cleverly ambiguous comment! 'You must meet him – somebody fetch the ugly little monster!' A slave dashed out. 'But now' – Nero laid a portentous, beringed finger on her arm – 'now I must tell you why I summoned you.'

'Your lightest whim is my heart's desire, Caesar!' The hair she didn't have tried to rise in apprehension. She showed no sign of it. Petronius would have been proud of her.

'The mob always want finer games, novelties – insatiable! And the cost! Heart-rending!' Nero sighed in theatrical despair. Victoria just stopped herself doing the same, in relief. 'But it came to me suddenly, how to entertain my people at no charge whatever to the state!'

'Noble thrift, Caesar!' the audience applauded. Anything that cut down the taxes . . .

He beamed round. 'Combats, not between expensive gladiators, but between amateurs!'

'Hmm. You don't mean just convicts, sire?' Victoria asked. That was normal. What new scheme was this?

'No, no, far better! The finest shows these days are provided by gladiatrixes. So thrilling!' He meant that he enjoyed watching women fighting and being hurt or killed. 'And it is only right, only just, that those who rule Rome should play their part in keeping Rome happy. So . . .' Pausing, he smirked round at the growing apprehension. 'I hereby decree that every senator must send one of his daughters into the arena as a gladiatrix – or his wife, if he has no daughter of a suitable age!' Apparently benign, in fact gloating, Nero studied the ghastly grins that tried to hide the senators' consternation. 'So simple, and so satisfying! Pretty girls, just dying to show how brave and strong they are. Just dying to!' He giggled again.

Nervous, sycophantic laughter rose through gritted teeth to applaud his atrocious pun.

Victoria could scarcely credit it. He was – he must be – driving them to revolt, piling tyranny on tyranny for his own pleasure, delighting in his absolute power. Like that speech in the Greek play she had seen last year: 'Whom the gods wish to destroy, they first make mad.' He was doing her work for her.

Nero waved his hands to silence them. 'But untrained girls

31

would give a terribly poor show. Comical, I'm sure, but not exciting. And very short, eh? So I sent for you to train them, Victrix.' Smiling, she hid her sudden rage. Drag her half across the world to train silly girls? What a flaming insult! 'You can use one of the courtyards here, so that I can come and watch sometimes, and you'll tell me if any of the girls aren't trying, so that I can have a little word with their fathers. You understand? All of you?' He looked round significantly.

'Now, Victrix, run along and have a chat to my little British bard. On you go!' He made a shooing gesture towards the exit, and turned back to Sporus.

Victoria bowed and walked through the high doorway.

Just beyond sight of the courtiers, a deep voice said, 'I greet you, Victrix.'

A slight, dark figure in a blue slave's tunic leant on a crutch before her. He was young, about the same age as herself, his left leg withered. His ears were hidden by flowing fair hair, but she knew that one was missing, as were two fingers of his left hand. She had been there when he was hurt, both times.

Victoria stared, and gasped. 'I don't believe it! Cram!'

She was moving forward to clasp his arms in greeting when his rigid face stopped her. 'What's wrong, Cram? Don't you know me? Your cousin Victoria?'

Her cousin bowed as if to a stranger, his tone flat. 'I know you, Victrix, Imperial Gladiatrix. Traitor!'

III

'Traitor? What do you mean?' Victoria demanded. 'How did you get here?'

'On a thread of gossamer the winds wafted me here!' Cram was sarcastic. 'I'm a slave, of course! Not a warrior, not a bard; a slave! But I can't complain, lady, can I? Or you'll have me whipped.'

'No!'

'No? How do I know what you'll do, Boudicca—' He broke off as she gripped his arm.

'Shut up! You'll get us both killed!' she hissed, aware of the senators only a few paces away, and the palace slaves, unseen but omnipresent as spiders. 'Call me Victrix, or Victoria! Or lady, if you must act the crawler!' She glanced round. 'Where can we talk in privacy?'

Her intensity overcame his sullen hostility. 'The garden. This way.'

They limped, both of them, to a bench in a grove of flowering trees. Heavy clouds loomed; despite the glow of her hurt and anger, Victoria shivered. 'Right. Speak in Iceni, so no-one will understand even if they overhear. Let's have it out, then. What's biting you?'

Cram glared bitterly at her. 'Boudicca our Queen laid a sacred command on you to destroy Rome, and you have lived here in the palace for months, and still Nero is alive!'

'So?' Victoria's expression was as grim as his. 'If I had killed him? What good would that have done? Executed I'd have been, and the next emperor just as bad! I'm working towards something far better, far more useful than getting myself killed just to swap tyrants! But if a traitor, a coward is what you think me, then tell me, Cram, glorious, heroic patriot, why is Nero still alive when you've been here for – how long? Why haven't you yourself killed him with a kitchen knife? Eh? No, not so easy, is it?'

They stared at each other. Slowly, Cram began to look doubtful. 'I thought . . .'

'You didn't think!' she snapped. 'It used to be you who told me to think. Still the person you knew in Britain I am, not stupid nor yellow nor false-hearted. When the task was laid on me you sneered, I remember! You thought I could not succeed. Well, I will! I am!' She looked round. Nobody was watching or listening. 'Go on sulking and sneering, all superior and betrayed if you like. Or start thinking!'

Cram studied her for a moment, and then stared at his feet. 'I'm sorry, Bou— Victoria. It's just – I hate being a slave!'

She couldn't help laughing. 'Nobody likes it, Cram! But I do understand. I had to become a slave to train as a gladiatrix, and whipped I've been more than once.'

'Heart's torment it is!' he snarled. 'To sing and make songs for Nero. To smile when he criticises, and thank him for his insulting, worthless advice. To praise his stupid poems and that breathy voice as if Rhiannon of the birds herself he was! Father's bard would have beaten me if I'd sung half as badly. Yet the other slaves envy me, having no hard work to do. They jeer at my lameness—' He stopped, and shrugged. 'Self-pity. I'll live.'

'How are my aunt and uncle? How did you come here?' Victoria asked.

'They're dead. Half Britain is enslaved. Father fought the slave-takers to let the rest of the village escape, and when he was killed mother seized his sword and went crazy, I'm told, so they killed her too. I wasn't there.' He sounded ashamed. 'Singing to the legionaries I was in Camulodunum – rebuilt already it is, and bigger, despite all I could do to sabotage it. A worthless cripple, they had always ignored me, but one day a message came that Nero wanted a British bard, and the trained ones being all dead I was the best they could get.' Cram's face was as sour as his voice. 'So they chained me and sent me south.'

'Smile, idiot!' Victoria warned him. 'Never show your real feelings!'

'Too late, cousin. Four times I've been whipped for it. I keep my mouth shut now.' He sneered in self-contempt, and there was a whine in his voice that hadn't been there in Britain.

'Wise you are, so,' she told him. 'But I'm doing more for Britain than you know. Seneca I've already dealt with. You know, the senator who helped cause Boudicca's rebellion? His nephew plotted against Nero, and I only needed to comment casually how astonishing that Seneca didn't know about it, for Nero to order him to kill himself. Ha! A whisper is strong as a shout, if you know the ear to drop it in. And it will be Nero's own turn next.'

'Truly?' His face was twisted with disbelief. 'How?'

'He's constantly trying to see how far he can go. He started out well, I believe, but these days he's becoming – vile isn't a strong enough word. Haven't you seen how his cruelty is driving people to revolt, to murder him like Caligula? And if the gods are with us—'

A ripping crash dazzled them, threw them to the ground in a stink of burnt air.

They pushed themselves up, dazed.

The Colossus, the supreme symbol of Nero's power, had been struck by lightning. Its golden head was dripping gold on the paving; an omen of disaster that no-one could hide.

'Indeed the gods are with us,' Cram breathed.

Two dozen Praetorians came racing up. 'What happened?' their officer demanded.

Wordlessly, Cram gestured at the ruined statue.

They stared, and then hid their shock with brutality as usual. 'Back inside, you! No slaves allowed out here except gardeners!' The centurion slashed at Cram with his vine-wood staff of office.

Instinctively, Victoria grabbed his wrist in fingers strengthened by hours of sword-practice and wrestling, twisting it rigid just this side of breaking, till the staff dropped. In the man's ear she snarled, 'He's with me.' She glared round at the soldiers, daring them to draw on her. 'And so is the Emperor.'

After a tense moment . . . 'Very good, miss.' The centurion's voice was thick with humiliation, his men bristling behind him. As she released him, he turned a dark glare on Cram. 'You're the British singer? I'll remember you, son. Oh, yes.' They marched off.

'Thank you very much.' Cram's voice was as sullen as the soldier's. 'Who was it a moment ago was talking about thinking? A good friend you've made me there, indeed you have.' He crutched off towards the palace without another word.

She cursed herself. She hadn't really helped. In fact, she had harmed Cram, made him a whole regiment of enemies. She really must start thinking before she acted! 'I'll get you out somehow!' she called. But how?

A month later, after reporting to Nero on the day's slapstick training session with her senators' daughters, Victoria heard a hiss. Someone was peering out of one of the small, camouflaged doors that led into the service passages which mouseholed the palace walls to let the servants move around without disturbing the court – not exactly secret, but not generally known except to those who used them.

'Cram! At last! I've looked for you and sent for you but nobody could find you – what's wrong?' Victoria leapt forward to support her cousin as his knees trembled. 'What is it? The Praetorians?'

'I hide, but once seen I'm easy to catch.' Cram's voice was husky. He was nursing his belly, and pulled aside the neck of his tunic to display blotches, both blue and older brown. 'Bruised all over I am. And a couple of cracked ribs. The Morrigan take them all!'

'What can I do?'

'Get me out!' He twisted his head to look up at her. 'Or had you forgotten me?'

'Never!' Victoria grimaced at his whingeing tone. 'I have been trying. You're like me, noticeable. Just running away would have to be very well planned. The Praetorians would hunt you hard, and they know I'm your friend, they'd search my house first, and question my servants and friends about hiding places. So I've spoken to the head steward about buying you out. He says as you're Nero's personal slave, you can't be sold openly, he can do nothing.'

'That's stupid! For a big enough bribe he'll fix anything, the slimy toad! He'd say I'd died, if Nero ever remembered me again!'

'Yes, I know, but he knows how rich I am, and how close we're linked, so he keeps saying he's afraid, putting me off and raising the price. I can't just take my sword to him, he's too important. And now that Petronius is dead I have no clout, except with Nero – and I can scarcely ask him to help me free one of his slaves! I have to negotiate, and I'm not good at that.'

'Please, Victoria! I've no friends to warn me or hide me, they're all scared or sneaks.'

His own bitterness would stop him making friends, she guessed. But she had to help. 'I didn't realise it was so desperately bad. I'll speak to Acte, she can maybe tell them to stop.'

'Her?' Cram spat. 'Soft as a cushion, when it's armour I need. I can't . . .' He drew a desperate breath. 'I can't last much longer. Soon I must run or die!' He glanced up sideways. 'And if they catch me, they'll torture me to find out who helped me. Of course I will try to keep quiet . . .'

'Are you blackmailing me?' she asked incredulously. Shameful!

Reading her disgust, he shook his head. 'No, no! But weak I am, weak, so far from my own gods . . . Oh, get me out! Please, Vicky!'

'I swear I will!' Her temper rising, Victoria tried to draw him along with her. 'Come on, we'll go together, now. I'll not let them hurt you.'

'Foolish! If the guards see me with you, will they not arrest me, charge me with stealing? The rest are all doing it. They'll plant something in my bed as proof and I'll be crucified, and you'll not be able to stop it. Just get me out! Somehow! Soon!' He crept off, hunched with pain.

Seething, Victoria squashed down her temper. That wouldn't help. Who could?

She went quietly, unostentatiously, to Vespasian's small town house, to find her best friend in Rome, Vespasian's mistress, her co-conspirator: Antonia Caenis.

'You look older. Bigger, more forceful. Harder.' Caenis poured wine for them both.

'Bossy, you mean? Not surprising, Caenis. And older, of course.' Relaxing with a sigh of pleasure into a comfortable chair on her friend's cool terrace looking north across the Via Sacra, Victoria poured the drop for the gods, and took a grateful gulp. 'Ahh, that's good! Fifty fights, at least one show a month, once, five – hard going, we've lost several good girls. Eleven wounds, cheating shipmasters and editors, pirates – they got a surprise! – insolent legion clerks, filthy taverns, bed-bugs, snakes and scorpions, and the girls falling ill or seasick or in love or too drunk to appear or demanding more pay – it puts years on you. I'm no longer a sweet little innocent.'

Smiling wryly, Caenis shook her head. Victoria was mistaken there; a fraction less naive, no doubt, but she would always be too straightforward and honest to master the labyrinths of nasty intrigue in the court. 'How many people have you killed?'

Everyone asked that. Victoria shrugged. 'A score or so in the arena, plus criminals, of course, though I don't normally have to do that these days, they leave that to the novices. But some will have died of wounds, that I never hear about. As I might have done with this leg. So I don't know, not exactly.' She didn't feel guilty, either. She fondled the golden torc at her neck, symbol of her hatred of Romans.

Perhaps that was what brought a memory drifting to her, from away back in Britain. Someone – her Aunt Aliss – saying, 'You don't enjoy killing. When you do, or when you don't care, your conscience will stop gnawing at you. Be glad of it, it shows you're human.'

She had stopped caring. Was she not human, then?

If the Romans didn't care about arena deaths, including her own, why should she?

Romans deserved to die. She hated them – most of them.

Maybe that was a reason for not copying them?

As Victoria sat silent, Caenis sighed, concerned. She was constantly surprised at the liking and respect she felt for this hulking, violent, uneducated young barbarian, a third of her own age. After all, Caenis herself was a rich, popular jewel merchant, cultured and elegant, with a shop in the expensive basilica of the Saepta Julia, acknowledged mistress of a famous general; she should by rights avoid a vulgar gladiatrix as she would a leprous drunk vomiting in the gutter.

She had accepted long ago that Vespasian could never marry her, however much they loved each other, for it was illegal for a senator to marry a freedwoman, and Caenis had been a slave, secretary to Antonia, the mother of Emperor Claudius.

But when Victrix – no, the girl wanted to be called Victoria now, outside the arena – when Victoria had suggested to her that they, two women in a male-run world, with oddly wide connections but neither noble birth nor political power, should try to wangle Vespasian onto the throne, astonishment had made Caenis listen. The frustration she felt that her beloved man's quality would never be rewarded properly, and her disgust at the Empire's decadence and corruption, had made her agree to assist the dangerous, fantastic plan. Victoria worked on the army, the base of real physical power, while it was Caenis's job to influence what the senators and rich equites, the people with political and financial power, said and thought. And somehow, incredibly, it was working.

'How are you getting on with the senators' daughters? Are they all ugly and clusmsy?'

'Well, of course! Ugly doesn't matter, but their fathers naturally send the stupidest and least attractive girls. Four are fine, they were in youth clubs already and actually learning some fighting, but most are pampered, sulky sapsies who burst into tears at the slightest smack,' Victoria snorted. She eased her leg after the hard afternoon's work. 'Waste of time, all of it. When they go in the arena, ten to one they'll forget everything, just shut their eyes and swing blindly.'

She sniffed in contempt. 'Talking about fighting, Caenis, what's all this about Hispania? On top of the rebellion in Germania – oh, did you hear about the letter the rebel there has sent Nero? I was there when it arrived. He accused Nero of murder, incompetence, decadence — that didn't matter, everyone just guffawed. But when the man said he was a rotten musician, Nero started screaming and foaming at the mouth!' They laughed together. 'No, the legions will deal with him. But there's this new problem away in the west. Nero's refusing to admit anything's wrong, but I hear the Spanish legion has declared Governor Galba Emperor.'

'Yes.' Caenis's smile was contented. 'And Galba's young friend Otho, Governor of Lusitania, is supporting him with another legion, and raising more. He's seized all the Spanish taxes, and he's offering the Praetorians a huge bribe to desert Nero. Over half the senators have written to him promising support, secretly, of course. He'll win, I'm sure of it. And so will we. Dozens of good omens for us. One of which stunned me, I must admit.'

'Truly? It takes a lot to throw you off balance.'

'Thank you, dear, but wait till you hear! Three days ago I was called from breakfast to speak to Nero. At the door, here. Driving the sacred chariot from the Temple of Jupiter! He said the god had told him in a dream to take it out and drive it to Vespasian's house.'

Victoria couldn't help gaping. 'What did you do? I mean — say the wrong thing, and he'd have killed you, and Vespasian, and half Rome!'

Caenis shrugged. 'What could I do? I passed it off lightly,

thanked him and Jupiter Optimus Maximus for this omen of success for Vespasian's campaign, and suggested he drive it round the Circus Maximus and back to the temple. And he did. But what an omen! One everybody noticed, of course!'

'People are pasting up notes against Nero in the Forum almost every night, accusing him of murdering his mother, all sorts of things – all true, but last year they'd not have dared. It's starting!' Victoria clenched fists and teeth in a grin of delight. 'He must go soon. And Galba's ancient, over seventy, he can't last long, and then . . . The legions are all talking about Vespasian.'

'So are the senators. They're beginning to listen to what I say, and what Sabinus says – he's Vespasian's older brother, the official head of the family, a lovely man but he knows Vespasian's the stronger character – anyway, he's campaigning for Vespasian too. And since everyone likes and respects him—'

'And you!' Victoria put in.

Caenis bowed acknowledgement, smiling. 'A few of the patricians and lots of the knights are starting to think of Vespasian as a real, possible contender for the throne, even though he's not from an old noble family.'

'Oh, you're doing so well! And you've heard why there are so many rebellions at the east end of the Mare Nostra – the prophecy that a man is coming from Judaea to rule the world? I didn't start it, but it fits Vespasian perfectly.' Victoria raised her glass. 'Fortuna!'

'Fortuna!' Caenis echoed her.

Her slave boy Lucius entered. 'Mistress, Flavius Sabinus and Flavius Domitianus are at the door.' He smiled at Victoria; they had met, very dramatically, during the great fire.

Victoria returned the smile, but in a distracted way. 'Vespasian's brother, and younger son? No, I mustn't meet them!'

'Why not?' Caenis raised a delicate eyebrow. 'I'll just be a moment, Lucius. Offer them wine.'

'The less contact people know we have, even Vespasian's family, the safer for us both. A casual word in the wrong place . . . That's why I've stayed carefully away. I only came today to ask your advice, but – another time, Caenis.'

Maybe asking Caenis how to help a slave escape wasn't the best idea anyway, now she thought of it; Caenis was Roman, after all.

'Write to me,' Caenis said.

'Yes . . .' Victoria considered. 'I have a lad, Oppio, who drives in with me. I'll send him to the fruit market every morning. If you send Lucius out then too, they can meet often, casually and innocently most days, and quietly pass over any note.'

'Use our normal code. Just in case. Any relative – like you, I haven't got any – means Vespasian, any unnamed friend means Nero.'

'And needing a holiday means come. Maybe I'll come in disguise.'

'You? In disguise?' Caenis gestured to Victoria's brilliant scalp. 'What as? Mount Etna? Or a bunch of lupins?'

Sticking her tongue out at Caenis's smile, Victoria dodged into a side room to avoid Sabinus and Domitian. The older man was short and solid, with the jutting jaw and flaring eyebrows Caenis said were the Flavian family's most striking features. He looked pleasant and capable, she thought, but she didn't like the looks of young Domitian, taller and slimmer than his stockily robust older brother Titus, and somehow less – less substantial. Pretty men with wonderful haircuts and gleaming smiles had brought her no luck in the past, and Domitian was a touch too wide across the lips and eyes. To most, it would give an impression of honesty; to Victoria, it indicated arrogant egotism.

Sabinus was grumping, 'And mind your manners!'

Domitian had always disliked Caenis, and had been rude to her in public – until his father heard about it. Now he protested, 'Of course, uncle!' all innocently insulted, shocked at the very idea. Yes, he was a sly one. He might just betray them out of spite, accidentally on purpose. Yes, better he didn't know about their friendship.

As she left, Victoria decided to start driving her chariot right in to work at the palace. If anyone complained, which was unlikely, she had two good reasons for it; her leg, which wouldn't carry her on imperial business, and carrying sacks of gear for her imperial trainees. Then, when people were used to seeing that, maybe a bigger bundle with a person smuggled inside it . . .

IV

Some days later, Victoria was summoned away from her training with the girls. Through an eerily empty palace – a few twitchy servants, almost no guards – she was led up to Nero's favourite room, a smallish, intimate dining room for only twenty-seven people, on the top floor, with wide windows to admit cool breezes. From sliding panels in the ceiling perfumes could be sprayed, and the floor revolved somehow to give diners a constantly changing panorama of the city in the fiery flare of sunsets which reminded Nero happily of the great fire.

The Emperor was pacing about nervously, almost alone. Sporus, encrusted with jewellery, was chatting with only three courtiers instead of the usual forty or fifty.

Nero leapt to greet Victoria. 'Victrix, how good are these girls you're training? They must be able to handle a sword by now? Of course they are. Because they may have to. Not that there's anything to worry about, of course. But you have heard about Spain?'

Warily, Victoria admitted to having heard some rumour about Galba.

'Such foolishness!' His chuckle was almost hysterical. 'He

and his troops are marching towards Rome. I shall go out to meet them, armed only with my lyre. I shall sing to them.'

To frighten the legions away, or charm them into submission? Victoria forced her face to show concern and enquiry rather than amazed ridicule.

'I shall remind them of their duty to their true Emperor, move them to tears' – very possibly, Victoria thought – 'tears of repentance!' Ah. Don't giggle! 'And then cheer them with comic songs I have composed about Galba.' Giggling himself, he sang a few lines of an extremely rude song to a well-known tune from the slums, before tossing aside his ivory lyre. 'Should I wear black, to show I'm mourning their disloyalty, or white for purity, like a candidate for consulship?' A vital decision.

Sporus looked round. 'You've dismissed the consuls, haven't you, sweetheart?'

'Can't trust anyone! All the army commanders too, I'll have them all executed, *and* the governors of the provinces!' Nero huffed in spiteful anger. 'Everybody exiled from Rome must die, they're all traitors. And the senators, too – I'll invite them to a banquet and poison the lot of them!' The attendant senators exchanged inscrutable glances.

'I did so want to be loved! But when I called the people to arms, nobody came!' His lip actually quivered, and then firmed into a petulant pout. 'So I've sent orders to let all the arenas' wild beasts out into the streets! I wish I could burn the whole place down again!'

His face changed, became dreamy. 'But when I am triumphant, I'll have a wonderful festival. I'll perform on successive days on my water-organ, flute, lyre, and bagpipes, and on the last day I'll put on a grand performance of the *Aeneid*, and dance the hero's role myself!'

What a drama queen!

'But now I must march against Galba,' Nero announced, all proud defiance. 'I can't trust the legions, so I'll make my own army! I've ordered the Praetorians to seize the biggest and strongest slaves from every household in Rome, and I'll take all my own slaves, even the women! And your girls too, Victrix! We'll cut their hair to look like men, and there's armour in the theatres – Amazonian shields and axes, lots of useful stuff!'

Stage equipment, Victoria thought; stiffened canvas armour, wooden swords covered with tinfoil. A crazy artificial army. Like his crazy dreams. He must know, surely . . .

A nervous freedman entered. 'Sire, the Senate has called an emergency meeting.'

The three senators slunk towards the door, murmuring, 'By your leave, Caesar . . .'

'I have not authorised this meeting!' Nero was imperious, but they simply scurried faster. His shoulders sank, and he shrugged helplessly.

Victoria wondered if she could escape too, but he clasped her arm. 'You are my only true friend, my defender, the only one I can rely on absolutely!' Ironic.

His voice sank to a whisper. 'Last night I gave my farewell performance for all my friends. All my friends . . .' His lips trembled again as his eyes drifted round the empty room. '*Oedipus in Exile* . . . You know how it ends?' He picked up his lyre; one of the horns was broken. His white, soft fingers caressed it, his eyes full of tears. 'Another omen . . .' Under his breath, he sang the last line of the part of Oedipus; 'Wife, mother, father, do my death compel!'

Like Oedipus, he had killed them all. Yes, he knew he was doomed.

Victoria cleared her throat. 'Sire, why not call your British bard to play to soothe you?' That would be the easiest way to find Cram in this huge building, and she could maybe slip him away with her when she left. Absently, Nero agreed, and she gestured to the servant to take the message.

Suddenly, Nero sank into a couch, sobbing, 'What will I do? What can I do?' His cosmetics were all smudged. 'Guard! Guards!' After some delay, a Praetorian appeared at the door. 'Send in your officer. No, all your officers in the palace. Hurry!'

The guard, astonishingly, hesitated before he saluted and left.

When Cram arrived, Nero just waved him to a stool. 'Play, play!' He himself went on with his nervous pacing and muttering.

'What's happening?' Victoria whispered as Cram tuned his harp.

50

'Everybody's leaving,' he murmured. 'Taking whatever they can carry. Ornaments, jewellery.'

Sporus tilted his exquisite head, considering. He nodded to himself, regarded his layered jewels with satisfaction, sighed, stretched sensuously and rose. 'Do excuse me a moment, beloved,' he cooed, and gave Nero a long, lingering kiss before wafting towards the door. There he paused a moment, to look back and wiggle his ring-laden fingers flirtatiously, lips smiling, eyes as full of hatred as Cram's. He'd never return.

Two officers of the Praetorians entered and saluted.

'Ah, yes. Er, I am going to – to Greece, or no, Parthia would be better, farther away . . . I need a guard to escort me, two hundred men. No, the whole regiment. Order my chariot.' They did not move. Nero's voice rose in pitch. 'Now! At once!'

With a dark, hidden glee the senior shook his head. 'Caesar, there are no men available.'

'But I must . . . I command you!'

They shrugged. 'Impossible.' Without permission, they turned and marched out.

'Insolence! But what can I do?' Nero wailed. 'What can I do? Oh, Isis, I'm done for!' He slumped on a couch, sobbing.

Cram began singing quietly in the Iceni style translated into Latin, a song dispiriting and deadly as a blade of ice:

'Bare to the sword's bright blade, the throat of the nation.
Poised on the knife's sharp point, the heart of the King.
Hungry the howl of the wolf, the croak of the raven,
Greedy the hounds of the gods pursuing their prey.
Lost is the laughter of life, the lightness of day.
Fear freezes fast in despair, the dark shadows gather.
Down swoops the vengeful night, the ultimate ending,
Bleak devastation, the horror of hoary winter.
Hopeless the fall of the star, the start of the dark.
Soul sinking lost in the ice, to vanish for ever.
Welcome the ruin of triumph, the triumph of ruin.
Death to the merciless murderer, arrogant tyrant,
Death to the man who destroyed the heart of my heartland.'

As if hypnotised, Nero cowered inside his purple tunic, staring out across the city in the last red glow of the sunset. Were there more torches than usual? More noise?

At length, Acte entered, pale and hesitant.

'What is it?' Victoria asked, when Nero sat motionless.

'Oh, Nero, dear, the Senate – the Senate . . . They've declared for Galba, all of them. And – and named you a public enemy.' Acte was so appalled she could hardly speak.

'What does that mean?' Victoria asked.

'It means they'll send lictors to arrest him, and flog him to death in the Forum with their rods.' Cram's voice was hoarse with triumph. 'He can be killed without penalty.

Anyone can kill him.' He looked significantly at Victoria's sword. 'Anyone.'

Nero was sobbing, great slobbery heaves, his make-up smeared and blotchy. Acte ran to take him in her arms, murmuring comfort as if to a hurt toddler. Over his head she lifted her soft, dark eyes to Victoria. 'What shall we do, Vicky?'

'Kill him,' Cram whispered. 'Kill him now. What are you waiting for? Do your duty!'

She should. She had every reason, every right. He had brought death to her and her loved ones. Her hand clasped the hilt of her sword.

But he was so pathetic – feeble, snotty, disgusting, but pitiful. And Acte, her friend Acte, was looking at her with absolute trust . . . 'No. Not now.'

Cram's face twisted in incomprehension, disgust. 'Then I will!' He snatched at her sword.

Automatically she swerved away. 'I said no!'

'Coward! Weakling!' he hissed. 'Queen Boudicca would be ashamed of you. I was right – traitor!' He spat at her. 'Why not?'

Why not indeed? She had killed so many men who deserved it less than he did.

But they were not in the arena; that made a difference, somehow.

Why?

Her mind felt muddled. She wanted to stay human. Or did

she? The last time she had shown mercy like this it had brought death to her family.

She needed more time to think.

She slapped aside Cram's hand that was reaching again for her sword. 'I'll get us out. That's the first thing. Away from the Praetorians. You think they'd be happy if I killed him? The way they feel about me? They'd kill me straight off – and you as well.' True, even if not her main reason.

'That doesn't matter!'

'It does to me!' She turned briskly away. 'Acte, you get Nero ready. Find him plain clothes, a hooded cloak, wash the paint off his face. Bring any money and jewellery you find to hand, but don't waste time hunting. I'll meet you at the outside door beyond the organ hall in ten minutes. Use the servants' passages as much as you can, you know them all. The outside door by the music hall, right? Hurry! The guards may be coming already.'

Looking quite intelligent in the urgency of the moment, Acte nodded and urged Nero out through a camouflaged service door. 'I didn't know this was here!' he protested, diverted instantly from his snivelling. 'It's dark—' The door shut off his comments.

'Cram, if you want to live through this night,' Victoria snapped, 'you go straight to that door, while I get my chariot from the stables. And pray to all the gods nobody sees us!'

She trotted, limping, along the echoing corridors. Only a

few muffled figures were scurrying about; enough to hide the Emperor's flight. She hoped.

Why in the name of all the gods was she doing this? Stupid, weak fool . . .

The vast marble stable for three hundred horses was almost empty. Five men were harnessing her ponies to a small, artificially decorated farm cart. Oppio was slumped nearby, sobbing, holding his head. The ponies were rearing, stamping and whinnying at the strange hands and words; that and the men's curses covered the noise of Victoria's footsteps.

Five men wouldn't stop for a single woman's telling, not even hers; they would fight. She didn't waste time or the advantage of surprise by challenging them; she attacked first, in relief that at least here she knew what she was doing and could work off her frustration. The two nearest went down fast. Heaving to his knees, Oppio threw an unsteady pitchfork which by luck stabbed the calf of a third. On the far side of the cart the others saw their mates fall, recognised Victoria, decided that even with their long knives, two and a half to her wasn't good odds, and fled.

Oppio spat on one of the dead men. 'Stinkin' rat!'

Victoria smiled at him, puffing; she was out of training, with this cursed leg! 'Well done, Oppio! Here, let me bandage that – hold the pad while I cut a strip off this guy's tunic. It's not too bad. Can you manage? Good lad! No, leave the ponies, we've got passengers. This cart's bigger, it'll carry everyone, and be less recognisable. Now there's a thought . . .' She pulled a long cloak off one of the fallen men to cover her head and clothes.

'Passengers?' Whatever her ploy was, Oppio was eager to help. 'Right, lady. I'll nip back for your chariot another time.'

Half an hour later, in a rainstorm, they were creeping past the Praetorian barracks to the Viminal Gate. From over west came the sound of rioting, but the trouble hereabouts had died, like the several scattered bodies they had passed.

Recovering from his collapse, Nero was dramatising his escape. 'The master of the world, fleeing in a cart! The mighty fallen to the gutter! What a subject for a tragedy!'

'Ssh! The gate's open and unguarded, like the park one; we can get past unnoticed,' Victoria hissed. She hopped down, handed the reins to Oppio – who was awed silent at being so near an emperor – and led the ponies forward to be certain of keeping them moving quietly.

'It should be shut at sunset!' Nero complained, peering forward.

Behind him, Cram had crouched in soggy, sulky silence all through the park and the city streets. Now he sniggered. 'So go in and scold them!'

Acte poked an elbow into his ribs. 'Don't speak to the Emperor like that!'

'What's he going to do to me – call the guard and have me executed?'

'Quiet!' Victoria snapped over her shoulder. 'Thank Fortuna for this rain, with that and the revolt they're all boozing inside the guard post, hear them singing?'

Suddenly Cram knelt up in the cart. 'Nero's here!' he yelled. 'Come on—'

For perhaps the only time in her life Acte moved fast without instructions. While Nero gaped and gasped in astonished terror, she simply pushed Cram over the side, to thud on his head on the muddy roadway.

As he struggled up, half stunned, Victoria dived back, grabbed him and shoved him against the cart, choking his dazed grunts of pain with a forearm. 'Shut up, Cram! Or I'll cut your throat!' She didn't think she could, actually, not to her cousin, but all that mattered was that he believed her for the moment. She turned from him to wave cheerfully over the cart to the soldiers peering out from the door of the guardhouse to see what the shout was about. 'We been celebratin' Nero going down!' she called, in her deepest voice. 'Get back up, you lummox, Mum'll murder you, the state you're in!'

She heaved Cram back up over the tailboard of the cart, to sprawl over Acte's legs. 'If he tries to yell again, stun him!' she hissed, clambering painfully up to retake the reins from Oppio. Noise didn't matter now; speed might, if the soldiers came out to investigate what Cram had shouted, and noticed the gaudy palace cart.

They didn't. Guffawing, they raised their mugs and wineskins. 'Good luck, son! Wait till we catch His blasted Imperial Highness, Galba'll pay well for him, an' strangle him for a traitor!'

'No,' someone else called, 'skin him alive!' Paying no attention to the cart rattling away in the darkness, they suggested other fates for the Emperor, increasingly painful, increasingly impracticable.

As their boozy voices faded, Nero was sobbing. 'Oh, gods, why do people hate me so?' The cart's clattering as it bumped across deep potholes was punctuated by his moans of grievance, while Acte tried to comfort him. Cram, to Victoria's relief, remained sullenly silent. At least the rain had stopped, and the half-moon dodging the clouds showed them bluish glimpses of the road, out through the suburbs, into the countryside.

Victoria had time to think. To fret. She had always hated being unsure of herself. Her present uncertainty worried her more than the darkness, the possibility of robbers or soldiers, the poor state of the road . . .

The cart crashed into an unseen hole, and lurched down as a wheel came off.

With a whimper of terror, Nero leapt out and vanished among the bushes. Acte scuttled after him. Cram started to laugh. 'Oh, brave Emperor! Brave Romans!'

'Oh, Morrigan take him!' Victoria snarled. She jumped down. 'Oppio, the path home's just a bit further. Leave the cart, lead the horses there, I'll bring Nero in.' Not waiting to see what Cram did, she slung Acte's valuable bundles far into the dripping bushes to lie hidden till she could collect them, and hurried off after Nero. This was ridiculous!

'Acte! Acte, where are you?' She forced her way towards the answering call, through a patch of brambles, till the hillside fell away unexpectedly, toppling her cursing down a steep slope to splash full-length into a gravel pit.

Nero was kneeling, scooping up the water for a drink. He tittered nervously as Victoria rose, filthy and angry. 'Have some of Nero's special brew!'

'I've had too much already!' Victoria huffed, abandoning her soaked cloak and wringing out her tunic. Too much of him, too! 'Come on. My house isn't far.'

'What's the use?' He sank down, sobbing, 'I'll be killed, or dragged in chains in Galba's triumph, and then strangled.' He sniffed, wiped his nose on his braided sleeve, and tried to control himself. 'I must deny them. Die nobly, by my own hand! Yes, I will! But' – anything to put it off – 'but first build me a funeral pyre.'

'The wood's all soaking, we'd never get it to light.'

Victoria's acid retort made Nero blink. 'Er, but with oil – no, there isn't any, is there? I must be practical.' There's a novelty, she thought in exasperation. 'So – dig me a grave. Yes, just a dirty grave. A fitting resting-place for such a wretch as I! I must die – and better here, among friends, than at the brutal hands of my foes.' He suddenly produced an ornate dagger from under his cloak, tried the point, winced and laid it aside. 'No, the fatal hour has not yet come!'

Acte was crying quietly. 'Yes, weep for me, my dear,' Nero told her, sadly. 'Lead the world to weep at my tragedy! You must sell those jewels you took, and arrange my funeral!' As she nodded, sobbing, he gave her extravagant instructions for his pyre, the speeches, the funeral offerings . . . In a twisted way, it was sensible; no-one else would risk annoying the new Emperor by showing any goodwill to the dead one.

At length, as the exaltation of sacrifice faded, he fell silent, drooping. His curls were uncurled in the rain, dribbling down his neck. Victoria, fuming wetly, was about to urge him to move on when he braced his shoulders and shook his head, showering everybody. 'Victrix, Imperial Gladiatrix, you are my guardian, my sword – you are accustomed to death. Set me an example of dying. Show me how easy it is!'

'What? You mean kill myself? Don't be daft!'

Disconcerted by her rude rebuff, he still nodded sagely. 'No, no, you are right. I must do this myself.' He scolded himself, 'Oh, what a coward I am! How ugly and vulgar my life has become! This is no credit to you, Nero, none! Pull yourself together!'

Above them, hooves rattled along the road. Nero cringed. 'What's that?'

Victoria shrugged, too cold and tried, dirty, aching and

disgusted, to try to soften the truth for him. 'Cavalry, it sounds like. Maybe somebody saw us leaving, and guessed where we'd go.'

'That's right.' Cram levered himself awkwardly down the hillside towards them. 'Twenty of them, at least.' He was grinning at Victoria. 'Well? What now, Imperial Gladiatrix?'

Nero raised his knife to his throat, but twice flinched at the prick. 'Help me – oh, help me!' he whispered.

Cram huffed in pure pleasure. 'Happy to, sire!' Before Victoria could stop him, before she could even consider whether she wanted to, he grabbed Nero's hand and shoved. The dagger slid into the side of Nero's throat. 'For Boudicca!' Cram hissed in Iceni. Blood gushed over his hand, blotching the Emperor's wet tunic with a redder dye.

Nero looked surprised; then his knees collapsed. He slumped sideways, onto one hand, down to his elbow. Acte sank to her knees, taking his other hand. For an instant, his eyes were desperately honest; 'I tried. I did try,' he whispered. Victoria's heart clenched painfully in unexpected, unwanted sympathy. Then his lips twitched back to his normal mocking smirk. 'What an artist the world is losing in me!' He fell back on the gravel, still looking astonished.

Oddly, it was again Acte who moved first, after what seemed an hour while they stood frozen by the body of the lord of the world. She lifted Cram's hand, still covered with Nero's blood, and kissed it. 'Thank you, oh, thank you, for helping Nero die swiftly!' Cram actually looked abashed.

Then she drew a deep breath and looked up trustfully. 'What now, Vicky?'

Victoria pulled herself together with a shiver. 'I'm chilled – we're all chilled. We'll go to my house and send someone to – to fetch him in. Galba will want to see him – his body.'

'I'll stay with him,' Acte said. 'It's not right to leave him alone.'

Cram stared at her, and at his hand, and at the corpse. He looked blank, almost lost. Victoria had to nudge his shoulder to get him to move, but as they started to push through the bushes to the path beside the river, he blinked at her, recovering his sense and triumphant hostility. 'It's done. I did it. It's – over. No thanks to you, weakling! Coward!'

Victoria turned aside from him and stopped, leaning on an alder tree, ready to vomit. She felt ashamed. It was true.

Though Cram had spoken in Iceni, Acte frowned at the cutting tone, and called from behind them, 'Never fear, I'll tell them you only did what he said.'

He laughed, answering in Latin, 'I have no fear, for I've done what the gods ordered!'

Horses galloped along the path towards them. 'There! Get him!' The cavalrymen surrounded Cram, their horses jostling him. 'Where's the tyrant?' someone yelled.

Unnoticed in her dirt and stillness beside the trees, Victoria could have stood and been ignored, but it never occurred to her. 'Halt there!' she bellowed, in a voice trained to cut through the roar of arena crowds. 'You want Nero? He's dead.' The only movement for a second was the trampling of the excited horses. She limped forward. 'Yes, dead. There he lies. His slaves here, Acte and Cram, helped him kill himself.'

They only hesitated for a moment before the commander gave a whoop of delight. 'Victrix! I know you! I won a hundred sesterces on you in the arena in Tunis. You're cursed lucky we're not Praetorians, eh? You two, dismount, tie the body over a saddle, bring the slaves back to the house. Victrix, mount up and ride in with us!'

Two hours later, Victoria settled into her bed, warm, dry and clean, with a hot meal inside her and a hot brick at her feet. The troopers had taken Nero's body away. Her ponies were in the stable, Acte's bundle under her bed. Nothing more to do for now.

Acte and Cram, as imperial slaves, had been returned to the palace; the officer had looked insulted when Victoria had hinted he might 'forget' Cram in return for a small gift.

Cram himself, accepting with a twisted smile the troopers' praise and envy at his deed, had only sneered balefully. 'I don't need your help any more, Victrix. My hand killed Nero. The Praetorians will love me now, I'll be a favourite of every soul in the palace, Galba will reward me!' She hoped he was right.

Judging by how he looked at her, his only feeling for her

nowadays was contempt. He had changed, lost the liking they had had before, in Britain. He had always hated Romans, and he seemed to see her as one now. Thank the gods she hadn't told him what she was trying to do for Vespasian!

Well, she had changed, too. Why, why, why had she not just killed Nero when she had the chance?

Oh, Bouda take it all for now! She yawned till her jaw cracked, and wearily blew out the lamp. The first step to Vespasian's crowning had been achieved. Deal with the next tomorrow. And Cram, and – and everything.

V

In August, tall but not outstanding in a man's dark-brown wig, tunic and cloak, feeling disconcertingly draughty round her bare knees despite the baking heat, Victoria stood at the back of the crowd in the Via Sacra to watch the triumphant parade as Emperor Galba went to his coronation. The three-hour procession wound slowly past, punctuated by a succession of dancers and bands of varying ability and unvarying din.

Four legions marched behind their sacred eagle standards carried by the tallest men of the regiments, sweltering in lionskins with the heads fastened to snarl over their helmets. The equites struggled with unaccustomed ceremonial armour and fractious horses. The senators processed solemnly in pairs, like pompous schoolchildren. Ten floats drawn by heavy horses displayed rather scanty trophies from the general's campaign and rule in Spain. Sullen 'captives' trudged in chains – bought slaves, Victoria had heard, or just Italian men kidnapped from towns north of Rome as Galba passed through; but at least not Nero, she thought in some satisfaction.

As the climax to the show, the new Emperor's gilded chariot rolled into sight, drawn by frothing black horses. She could see the old man clearly over the heads in front of her, panting with excitement, his puffy face red-painted in the traditional style. A tall slave held a laurel wreath high over Galba's head; from time to time he was supposed to whisper, 'Remember you are mortal!' to reduce undue pride – but she doubted if that tradition had survived the last four Emperors.

Beside her, an elderly woman was hoarse with cheering, but still voluble. 'At snotty last! Oo, don't look healthy, do he? Terrible fat, look at his belly wobble, an' them baggy eyes!'

'Gouty, they says, hands an' feet both, all swole an' can't bear nothin' t' touch 'em, can't wear shoes even,' her neighbour commented, tossing her last flowers at the Emperor, and blowing kisses to the rearguard cohort marching behind the chariot. 'That's why 'e's sittin', see? Can't even stand, not long. Funny t' see all them skinny Spaniards as 'is bodyguard, 'stead o' Praetorians. But I 'ears as 'e only trusts them as 'e brung with 'im. 'E's sacked 'alf the Praetorian officers, an' all the marines, they been fightin' these new lads an' riotin' all over, shockin' bad round our way. Scared to go out me door! My niece Fastia, her tripe stall got smashed t' kindlin' ten days back, poor lass. My ol' man says . . .'

The final band drowned what her old man said, and as everyone rushed off towards the Forum to grab seats for the traditional feast that would soon be laid out there for thousands of people from the city and the surrounding countryside, Victoria slipped away up the side street to Caenis's house.

She told the porter, 'Gaius Torinus to see Antonia Caenis.

66

A matter of Mount Etna.' Not recognising her, he rather suspiciously showed Victoria to a bench in the atrium, beside the small pool with its pretty antique statue of a nymph, and sent Lucius for his mistress. To Victoria's satisfaction, Lucius did not know her either.

Caenis did. 'Torinus?' she asked politely, as she came in, blinked, and talked on smoothly. 'Ah, yes, Mount Etna, I remember.' She beckoned towards the terrace. As soon as they were alone, she murmured gently, 'You make a very good man, my dear. The wig is excellent, and you're scarcely limping. It's mending? No? Still bothering you? How annoying! Sit down. I've had your messages, and I don't think anyone has noticed them.'

'No, Oppio's a smart little squirt, though he looks as thick as Tiber mud, which is handy. You'd think he was a frail brat without enough thoughts to keep his ears apart, but he handles my horses like a veteran, he's longing to be a racing driver. He got the wig for me – told the hairdresser his master was going bald, and you Romans do so despise that, the man wasn't at all surprised that his customer wanted to stay anonymous. I came as quickly as I could, your note said you needed a holiday really soon. What's so urgent?'

'Two things.' Caenis fingered a silver and jet earring in a rare sign of perturbation. 'I've heard murmurs that you're possibly a traitor. Nothing definite, you understand, but worrying. Galba is quite ruthless, executing people without even a mock trial. Worse than Nero. He heard that people are taking about Vespasian as the next emperor, just a hint of a rumour about gossip, but instantly he sent murderers to kill him.'

'What?' Victoria stiffened in alarm.

'Oh, they were caught and executed without publicly implicating Galba, but the legions know and they're seething. He did us a good turn without meaning to.'

'Is Vespasian going to claim the throne?' Victoria asked eagerly.

'Not yet. His latest letter yesterday – in code, of course – says he has ordered his men to swear allegiance to Galba, as is his duty. He's not going to rush into anything without full preparation and lots of support. Most of Judaea is reasonably calm now, and he's talking to all the local kings. Titus is enormously useful, not just with the army, he seems able to win over all the local politicians from Libya to Armenia. He has the knack of bribing them, promising gifts and favourable taxes in return for their support, without insulting their pride. That would put their price up! Don't look disgusted, dear, it's just the way politicians work. Some politicians, anyway. Everybody in Rome and many of the provinces knows and respects Sabinus, of course. Even young Domitian is making friends with all the right people here. He can be charming when he cares to take the trouble.' Caenis's tone was caustic.

'Why does he dislike you so much?'

'He knows his father's marriage wasn't a love match, just a family arrangement organised by his grandfathers, but his mother was a pleasant, kindly woman, and Domitian resents that Vespasian could love an old freedwoman like me more than he did his wife.'

'I see.' Victoria nodded.

Caenis's lips quirked ruefully at her young guest's unconscious insult. 'But that's not important here and now. We're still left with your problem, Victoria.'

'I've sensed something,' Victoria said thoughtfully. 'I've been visiting the editors about work when the Amazons get back, but they're reserved, edgy, promising nothing. And Oppio says I'm being followed. I think it's my cousin Cram. He's a palace slave, the one who actually killed Nero. I'm afraid he hates me. I'll not bother you with the reasons, but he could be telling people that I worked against Nero, and may be plotting against Galba too. Thank the gods I never mentioned Vespasian to him, and I hope he doesn't realise what I'm up to. So I'm being very, very good, everything open and honest, and staying well away from you. I talk to soldiers home on leave, of course, but I'm still careful. But when your note sounded so pressing – well, I thought I'd vanish among the crowds coming in for the triumph today.'

'You must go further than that, my dear. For the present, at least.'

'For the present?' Victoria asked. 'What's happening that I don't know about?'

'You know Nero spent every last copper, and the Treasury is empty as a drum. Galba can't pay the German legions the bonus they're due for putting down the last rebellion there. He's even refusing to pay the Praetorians' bribes that Otho promised them for supporting him. "I choose my friends," he says, "I do not bribe them!"'

'Ahah!' Victoria said, in satisfaction. 'I've noticed they're not the usual chirpy little cherubs, but I thought it was just the trouble with the Spaniards.'

'They're near mutiny, I hear,' Caenis agreed. 'The whole city's unhappy. Galba is frantic for money, so this is the other thing I have to tell you. He plans to seize back all the gifts Nero ever made to anyone, even if they've been sold on. And your little villa—'

'Will be one of the first to go. Of course. Cram will see to that. Thanks for the warning.' Victoria sighed. 'Pity. I like it. But these seizures will turn even more people against Galba, eh? So some good's coming from it. Maybe Vespasian will return it to me later? But if there's no money, how will he manage when he takes over?'

Caenis laughed. 'He's the son and grandson of bankers and tax-gatherers. If he can't run the Empire at a profit, my dear, nobody can!'

Lucius brought out a tray with iced wine and figs.

Smoothing her fine silvery gown, Caenis waited quietly as he served them, bowed politely, and left.

'Yes, an excellent disguise!' Caenis murmured. 'So what will you do? Where will you go?'

'Well.' Victoria had been considering this. 'You remember my friends who started up the Amazons with me? Divina died of a belly wound in Egypt, but Africa took the girls on when I was recalled. They're due home soon, and I've been looking for a house with a big yard for a palaestra for us. There's a burnt-out warehouse and goods yard near the Ostia road, four miles or so from the Lavernalis Gate. I'll buy it and get the builders in right away. And in the meantime, I'll go back to Pompeii. My leg's not mending as it should.' She snarled in irritation. 'Aagh! I don't understand it. I normally heal like a dog, fast and clean. This has been getting better, like today, but then breaking down again, over and over. Manny, our physician in the training school in Pompeii, is the best ever. So I'll go and see him.'

Caenis nodded approval. 'Stay with Julia Felix.'

'What? That snooty old witch? She'd no more let a gladiatrix stay in her posh mansion than eat catshit.'

'Your language, dear!' Caenis scolded, laughing. 'I thought with no bad influence from your Amazon friends these days, you'd be more refined and lady-like!'

'Lady-like? Me? No chance!' Victoria blew a ripe raspberry.

Caenis laughed again, shaking her head. 'No, Julia Felix

71

has changed since you met her. She says she's old enough at last not to worry any longer about her reputation, anything outrageous she does will be put down to senility, so she's recalling her youth, when she was the prettiest and most scandalous girl in Italy. She's renting half her house to a young men's club, with a standing invitation to all their parties as part of their rent, and having a wonderful time again. She'll welcome you with open arms, I promise you. Just don't blow raspberries at her! Nobody will look for you there, or, if they did, would dare arrest you in her house, she knows too many of all the magistrates' secrets. You can drop out of sight for a while, and when you return it may all have blown over.'

'Or Galba may have!'

Buying the warehouse took far longer than Victoria had expected; she wasn't used to lawyers – 'Nit-picking twisters!' Then she didn't trust the builders to work unsupervised – 'Useless layabouts!' When it was finished, though, it would be excellent. The old warehouses were to be converted into a pleasant house on two levels, its windows all looking inwards onto a sheltered garden, with twenty small bedrooms for the fighters. The big yard at the side had a wide gateway for carts; Victoria ordered a strong gate, with a little wicket door with a grille in one leaf. A new kitchen and a small private bathhouse beside the well – she remembered how grateful she had been for that while she was training – would still leave plenty of space for exercise.

Frustrated and fuming, she welcomed the Amazons' arrival in September. They drove their wagon into the new yard and tumbled out to hug Victoria, shouting greetings. 'Hail, Victrix! – We've walloped the world! – Champions! – The presents we got in Antioch! You left too soon! – See my bracelet – amber, not glass – from a fan in Ephesus! – Good to be home, though, see the Blues again! – Oh, Mars, what a big place! Bags I the corner room!' They raced off to explore their new home.

Tall and languid as always, bandages on her neck and left arm half hidden by her stacked necklaces and bangles, Africa exchanged news with Victoria over a cup of watered wine in a corner of the yard pleasantly shaded by an ancient cypress. 'Those silly novices from Palmyra, I said they were too conceited to listen, strolled out to their first fight as if it was a party and – *poof*, all three gone within thirty seconds. No loss – not like Gladia, she was killed in Antioch. And just after you left, Hydra flirted off with a silk merchant – a gorgeous guy, I nearly grabbed him off her! Julia lost a hand, but only her left, and she's got a fancy clip made to hold her shield – she'll do. We lost Tyrannix in Moesia – remember her? Always thrust out too far? Another one that wouldn't listen. But we picked up six good girls, strong, fierce shepherd lasses, used to defending their flocks from bandits and bears and wolves – two volunteers, four from big debt-ridden families, sold off

73

cheap as slaves by their fathers or uncles. I've said we don't have slaves, we'll free them, and they're so grateful it's embarrassing. Parmenia's the biggest and strongest girl I've ever seen, I'll swear she could hunt a hippo alone; she'll carry secutor's armour no bother. And Nerva can use a spear with either hand; once she learns how to handle a net, she'll be a splendid retiarius.'

'Never as good as you, naturally!'

'Impossible!' Africa grinned. 'We've made a piled profit, Victrix. I've got bankers' drafts for thirty-eight thousand sesterces, after all pay and expenses.'

'Good, this place has cost a mint! We can afford a good bonus, then?'

'Depends on your costs here, I suppose, but I thought up to a thousand sesterces each, for the girls who've been with us longest.'

Victoria looked doubtful. 'Will they stay?'

Africa laughed, her teeth startling white against her wide, rouged mouth. 'Where would they go? Who else would take such good care of them? Where else could they earn such good money? They'll invest some – if they're sensible – and buy fancy armour, and likely party for days . . . but they'll trickle back, all worn out and hungover, and I'll sober them! You go off to Pompeii and get that leg mended, give Manny my regards, and don't worry about the Amazons. The news of that bonus will bring in dozens of volunteers. I'll keep the builders working and start training as soon as we can.' She indicated a few travel stains on her tunic. 'And get some new clothes; I look like a tramp.'

'You shouldn't wear yellow to travel in. It's not practical.'

'I like gold.' Smugly, Africa chinked her bangles, her eyes merry. 'Who doesn't? When will you be back?'

'When I can. Maybe for the Saturnalia. I'm not in favour just now—'

'They've heard about you promoting Vespasian?'

Victoria's jaw dropped. 'You know?'

'Slow, you were always slow, girl!' Africa grinned. 'You think we don't pay any attention to what the boss does and says? Don't worry. We agree with what you're doing, those of us who care, and the ones who don't won't gossip. Not if they know what's good for them! But they like you too much to get you into trouble anyway, gods know why!'

'Oh, you big black rainbow!' Victoria hugged Africa while the black girl laughed.

Smarandax was equally supportive, in his waffly, chinless way. 'Don't worry, mistress, I'll move everything to the new house, leave nothing here except the walls, nothing.' He looked round his beloved garden and sighed before firming his shoulders again. 'Perhaps – er – yes, we'll even take the roses. Don't you worry about a thing!'

Smiling in the doorway behind him, Mira nodded briskly. 'We'll see to it all. Don't worry, lady.'

Everyone was telling her not to worry. It was worrying.

★ ★ ★

At last, in mid-October, Oppio, in a smart new tunic, drew rein outside the door of Julia Felix, one of the richest and most respected ladies in Pompeii, in whose mansion Victoria and Caenis had first met.

Victoria climbed down, weary and stiff; her leg was bad today. In the reception room, between two scented braziers, Julia Felix was sitting in a cushioned chair, stiff, straight and chilly as an icicle. 'Victrix. I had heard you were dead.'

Oh, curse Caenis! But was that a twinkle in the old lady's eye? Victoria bowed politely. 'Yes, Julia Felix, I heard that too. But I didn't believe it.'

The crinkle at the corner of her hostess's eye grew deeper. Her lips twitched. Suddenly the ice melted in a snort of laughter. Victoria bowed again, more deeply, smiling. 'Lady, you are generous to receive me as your guest. Please accept this small gift.' Her hostess received the carved ivory panel of Venus and her lover Adonis with a chuckle of bawdy delight. 'I'll keep quiet while I'm here – I don't want to embarrass you—'

A skeletal raised hand stopped her. 'Don't bore me, girl, life's too short these days. When you've bathed, come and tell me how Nero died – I hear you were actually there? And give me all the latest tittle-tattle about Tawdry Towers!'

That evening, rested after her tiring drive, Victoria brought her hostess up to date with the scandal. Skinnier and frailer than ever, but waspishly alert, Julia Felix was, as always, richly jewelled and gowned, though in brilliant crimson and blue instead of her former restrained shades. It seemed to symbolise her new, liberated way of life. Victoria found that as well as respecting the old lady, she now liked her enormously.

Julia Felix was maliciously delighted with Nero's dying performance. 'Couldn't even kill himself – typical! There's not a soul mourns him.'

'Acte?'

'Huh! That girl would break her heart for a pet lark dying . . . Petronius might have.'

'Mourned Nero? I doubt it!' Victoria snorted. Then she considered more carefully. 'Well. Maybe he would. How did he die? Caenis wouldn't talk about it.'

'She wouldn't. It upset her badly, though we'd all expected it. Tigellinus finally produced proof that Petronius was involved in a plot. Forgeries, of course; but Nero panicked, wept for being betrayed by his dearest lover, and ordered Petronius to kill himself. Nincompoop!' The old lady snorted contempt. 'That night Petro held a party, with all his friends who dared to attend. Lots of laughter, marvellous food, fine wines, exquisite music – which made a pleasant change for them all; and at midnight he led them all into a room where he'd had a hot bath filled, climbed in, and had his physician open his veins. Then, while the water turned red, he dictated a letter to Nero.'

She considered Victoria, and nodded. 'Yes, I believe I can

trust you. A friend sent me a copy. It's hidden in that end pigeonhole, inside the scroll on Etruscan grammar – so dull, nobody would dream of opening it. Yes, that one, go on, girl.'

Victoria unrolled the long scroll till a smaller curl of papyrus fell out. Chuckling, Julia Felix beckoned her to hand it over. 'Pin back your ears! "To the Emperor Nero, hail and farewell. I received your message with no surprise, and with relief, rather than dismay. I have long known that your sordid spymaster Tigellinus hates me, because I despise the scabby scoundrel and oppose the excesses to which he has urged you ever since he poisoned his predecessor and encouraged you to murder your mother. You deserve each other." '

'Oh, Bouda!' Victoria's face was full of appalled joy. 'What did Nero say?'

'Too shocked to speak, girl! Ssh! Don't interrupt! "I can almost forgive you, Caesar, because you were badly brought up. Few toddlers see their family murdered and their mother exiled, and are left in the care of the murderer. Few sixteen-year-old boys have a mother who will poison their stepfather and half-brother to steal an inheritance for them. I can almost forgive you for ruining the Empire, leaving it in the hands of rapacious slaves and freedmen – your predecessors set you the example for that. I can almost forgive your callous relish of cruelty and decadence – they run in your family. I can almost forgive your burning of Rome, your vicious treatment of the Jews you blamed for it, and the legal and personal atrocities

78

you commit to extort money for that gaudy carbuncle, the Domus Aurea. I can even bear your vulgar taste in clothes and lovers, despite all my efforts to educate you." '

Victoria was laughing so hard, she nearly fell off her couch. Twinkling, Julia Felix continued. 'I'll miss out the next bit: a list of all Nero's girl – and boyfriends, and the nasty tricks he got up to with them – scores of them, it goes on for ever! Now, then – ah, yes – "These, however, are all frivolities beside the one thing which I cannot forgive you: your assaults on the Muses. Any normal boy of ten could write superior verse – I cannot call it poetry – and perform more skilfully on your over-decorated, under-tuned lyre. Your latest fad, the water-organ, pollutes the air with its disgusting groans. Worst of all, though, has been the torture of what you mistakenly call singing. The happiest part of dying is the knowledge that I shall never again have to pretend to enjoy that grating whine. I thank you most heartily for my release to the comparative ecstasy of Hades." '

Julia Felix tossed the scroll to Victoria. 'When you can stop sniggering, put that back for me, girl. Well! Nero always wanted new experiences.'

'He got one then! Oh, how like Petronius! Oh, I wish I'd been there!'

'So do I!' Julia Felix sighed in regret. 'Yes. A wicked tease, Petro; in many ways no better than his master, but clever and amusing, and a good friend to those few he respected. He even thought to free his slaves, and told them to run in case Nero took out his anger on them. Nero destroyed his house, but the slaves all escaped.'

'Like Sporus,' Victoria commented. 'I didn't realise how much he hated Nero, till I saw him kiss him before he left, with such a – a creamy smile.'

'You can't blame the boy, after the way Nero treated him. But Galba is just as tyrannical, I'm told, and not even ornamental. Nero at least tried to encourage the arts. What does Galba encourage – gluttony and greed? Where will it all end?'

To that question, Victoria could not venture any answer. Where would it all end? Would her leg ever heal properly? Would she ever return to the arena? Would she find a cure for her shocking softness? Where would *she* end?

VI

Manny had bought himself free from the old gladiatorial school, and developed a very popular practice among the rich and powerful of Pompeii. Even with Julia Felix's influence, it was noon next day before such an esteemed physician deigned to respond to Victoria's request for a visit.

The tall Jew was yet more stately than he had been before, as he examined her leg thoroughly. 'Yes. Yes. Bad. Very bad.' He probed and poked agonisingly from her calf to her hip, puncturing the weeping swelling, and squeezing till it oozed yellow pus, at which he sniffed deeply, his nose twitching, before standing up, wiping his hands on a scented cloth and frowning. 'You have fever, growing for six or ten days while a boil gathers here. Fomentations raise it, make it burst, clear it up for some days, and then the fever returns. Over and over, yes? Yes. Your thigh has poison deep inside, Victrix, right beside the bone. The gods favour you that you have withstood it thus long. A weaker man would be dead – or woman, very well, do not interrupt me! Any other surgeon would have to cut the leg off to have any hope of saving your life. You are fortunate that I am here.'

'True, Manny.' With pain, fever and apprehension, Victoria's head was swimming too much for her to joke at his pomposity as she would have done when he was just the physician of the palaestra where she trained.

He peered down at her over his hooked nose, smugly smoothing his fine linen tunic. 'I am nowadays called Glaevius Emmanus.' He waited until she nodded acceptance of his freedman's name. 'Yes. I must extend and cleanse this wound, remove the rot.'

'You mean cut it?' Victoria grimaced.

'How else?' Manny's – Emmanus's – bushy eyebrows rose.

Pain, she could stand – wounds in hot combat were an accepted risk; but the thought of a cold opening of her flesh made Victoria's scalp creep.

Emmanus looked down at her with stern sympathy, and instructed the steward, 'Fetch rope, to tie her down and hold her still.'

'You'll not need that,' Victoria protested.

'Indeed? We shall see.' He took a flask from his slave boy. 'Drink this, Victrix, while I make my preparations. It will deaden the pain somewhat.'

It did, at least enough for her to practise the trick she had learnt long ago. She managed to lie unmoving on a sunlit bench in the garden, stuffing the pain away into a black bag in her mind and ignoring its shrieking in there. It took all her self-control, but the rope was not needed.

Emmanus sliced down with his small steel scalpels, carving

deeper and deeper into her thigh until bone glinted in the depths, while his assistant held the edges of the cut wide with hooks. For ten eternal years, it felt like, he snipped at the disgusting mess he uncovered and swabbed it with wine. Then he poured in a handful of squirming bluebottle maggots. 'These will eat away any dead flesh.' He dusted the wound with powdered cinnamon, bandaged it – inserting a silver pipe to let it drain – and slowly released the tourniquet. Finally he stood back, washing his hands with scented water and more wine, and nodded grudging approval. 'You bore it bravely. Well done.'

'It will heal?' Victoria murmured.

'Of course!' He radiated haughty confidence.

For two months Victoria remained in the house of Julia Felix while her leg slowly mended. The members of the men's club and their girlfriends were frequent visitors, eager to chat with this celebrity of the arena. Kinder than her malicious reputation gave her credit for, her hostess also often sent slaves to read to her and play music or draughts, or herself entertained the patient with amusing, mischievous gossip.

However, Victoria refused to lie still. 'I'd go crazy!' Within six days she was up, hopping rather shakily with crutches round the house and then with slowly growing agility through the streets, renewing acquaintance with the local editors for future shows, admiring the final repairs after the earthquake some years before, accepting invitations to rowdy or elegant dinners with fans.

She had been more run-down than she had realised, and the wound left a frighteningly deep scarred hole and a shocking weakness in her leg muscles. However, as soon as possible, she limped to the nearest palaestra and demanded to train there every morning. Though the lanista disapproved of gladiatrixes, he appreciated what his men could learn from her in ring-craft. She forced her leg to hold her, till she could hobble with a single crutch and then with a staff.

In the afternoons, even if it was cold and raining, she usually went out driving with Oppio. 'Your hands are not as strong as mine, boy, but you've got a good feel for the horses' mouths, and you seem to understand them,' she told him.

Guiding the ponies round a corner at a canter, his hands light and steady on the reins, the boy frowned absently. 'Aye, of course, lady.' As if driving was as simple as walking. Cheeky brat! Grinning, Victoria ruffled his tousled head, surprised by the affection she felt for him. For her, horses were big stupid brutes. Driving was better than riding, but though she was good at it, she didn't find it as natural as Oppio clearly did. Yes, she had a good lad here.

Cautiously-worded gossipy letters from Caenis to Julia Felix brought news. In October, ' "My friend Flatulus—" ' The old lady stopped reading. 'Flatulus? Who's that?'

'Galba.'

'Ah. How suitable. "Flatulus found the grey dog he had lost." Grey dog? Your Villa Glauca, girl? Yes. Ah, well. That's emperors for you. "Sabinus tells me his friends in the legions in Germania are homesick. To comfort them, Galba's sending them a new commander, his old friend Vitellius, a close companion of the last four Emperors." '

'Homesick? More likely unhappy at not getting their bonus,' Victoria suggested.

'Yes. And Vitellius won't help.' Her hostess chuckled scornfully, and sniffed in contempt. 'Old? Ancient. He's older than I am. And a toady. He was in the invasion of Britain, senior to Vespasian, but left early – too dangerous, and too cold for his tender little senatorial tootsies!'

'He'll love warm, sunny German winters, then!'

'It couldn't happen to a more deserving person.' Julia Felix's grin was malicious. 'Close companion, indeed. One of Tiberius's little playfellows when he was a boy, very enthusiastic too, and then progressed to be a bosom friend of Caligula; you know the type that means? Yes. Nearly eighty, enormous debts – if his creditors dare demand repayment, he accuses them of treason so that he'll not have to pay them while they're on trial, and the lawyers' fees ruin them anyway. If Galba did send money north, the legions wouldn't see a sniff of it – don't snigger, girl, you know what I mean! An arrogant aristocratic snob, Vitellius is, with less military ability than my cat. And a glutton, that's why Galba appointed him, he thinks men who think so much of their bellies don't think of plotting. He's wrong – I mean, there's himself, for one! There'll be serious trouble up north soon.'

Victoria smiled gently. Good.

Then her jaw dropped, as Julia Felix glanced slyly sideways at her and added, 'Vespasian will be far better.'

'Ve-Vespasian?' Victoria could barely breathe.

Like Africa, the old lady chortled. 'I'm no fool, girl. And Caenis is a good friend. Of course I know what you're doing! I'm helping all I can, talking to my friends – and I have hundreds. But it has to be slow, delicate, in case I alert Galba's spies. I wish you luck. I wish us all luck – we'll need it!'

In November, Caenis wrote: 'The jewel trade has fallen off badly these days, there are so many disturbances round the Forum, fights and riots and rumours of worse to come. Sabinus is tearing the hair he hasn't got. However, my cousin is hoping to move to Rome soon, as she thinks her affairs will be settled fairly quickly.' That meant Vespasian, sensibly lying low till he had everything organised before he made his move for the throne. 'Galba thinks the troubles are because he has no heir, and plans to adopt one. Imperial tradition! I'm betting on Piso, a nice young man, very popular in the Senate; but most of the sesterces are on Otho. Everyone knows he's due a reward for helping Galba gain his throne. Nonetheless, he's a knight, not a patrician like Piso – and going bald, poor man, even though he's only in his middle thirties; a terribly bad mark against anyone, however excellent his toupée. The weather, both meteorological and political, is so nasty, I think I'll need a holiday fairly soon.'

That was a summons: Victoria nodded to herself. It was up to her and Caenis to stop this nice young Piso. Otho sounded a better bet, easier to get rid of later.

In December, Emmanus grudgingly admitted that Victoria was mended enough to leave his care, but Julia Felix urged her to stay on for the Saturnalia. 'Such fun, dear! The festivities last a full seven days now. So many of the eastern religions celebrate the winter solstice – Mithras and Ahura Mazda and a couple of the Egyptian gods as well as our own Saturn – you can always find somebody having a party. Everybody's on holiday, even the law courts shut, nobody does any work except foodsellers and entertainers. You must stay, girl, I'll have the merriest parties in the Empire, you'll really enjoy yourself!'

So she did, and she did, and she did.

Everyone had new clothes, for a start. The local tailors remembered Victoria well; she had started a brief fashion for bright checks or stripes, and several had material left over which they were overjoyed to make up for her.

Everybody gave presents. Victoria delighted Oppio with a red tunic and also a knife in a red leather sheath; as a free man – well, free boy – he was allowed to carry a weapon. She gave

Julia Felix a traditional figurine of Saturn, but carved in onyx, not the more usual pottery. She received many gifts, too, both surprising – like the talking parrot from one of the young men of the club – and traditional: from Oppio a small candle, the kind exchanged by slaves who had very little money, and from Julia Felix a huge pink one as big as her leg, in a very rude shape. They were used to light the revelry.

Victoria couldn't bear to see the parrot in its small cage, so she let it fly free. To everyone's pleasure it decided to stay, perching decoratively on the roofs and coming down to take corn from their hands and bathe in the atrium pool. 'Though what it will do to the rosebuds in spring, I shudder to think!' Julia Felix remarked drily.

For days the house slaves were busy bringing in sheaves of ivy and holly to tie with red ribbons onto all the statues and pillars. The house smelt divine, of spices and hot honey, as the cooks prepared special spicy Saturnalia cakes stuffed with dried fruit soaked in wine.

Julia Felix's family all came to visit in turn, bringing wives and husbands, children and friends. Victoria stayed in her room to avoid them till Julia Felix called her out, chuckling. 'Coward! They're gone! That parrot chased them – it nipped Julius's finger till the poor soul almost wept! But I never let the family stay more than half an hour anyway – pompous nitwits. I tell them I'm old and tire easily, and they can't argue, in case I disinherit them.' She twinkled naughtily.

'Oh, you liar, lady! You can dance us all off the floor,' Victoria scolded.

'No, girl, no longer. Once, yes, but not these several years.' Julia Felix sighed, but brightened. 'But I can still keep my end up with storytelling.'

'You know more gossip about more senators and their youthful pranks than anybody in Italy.'

'Well, I was often the prank, girl! Come along, let's go through to the club for some fun.'

On the third day, the social order was turned topsy-turvy. Slaves were allowed to wear their masters' clothing, and were waited on at mealtimes instead of doing the serving, in memory of an imaginary golden age of equality under the rule of Saturn. 'Some slaves take advantage of the chance to get their own back for beatings and injustice,' Julia Felix commented. 'It's all supposed to be forgotten next day, but with a bad master that's not likely. However, they may think it's worth it. Of course, a real brute won't do it at all.' She sniffed contempt.

Her own slaves liked and respected her as a good mistress, despite her tetchiness. The maids borrowed old gowns from her huge clothes-press, and as always chose the house steward as an extremely self-conscious Lord of Misrule. In the dining room the servants climbed up to lie round on the couches, fidgeting uneasily to arrange the cushions under unaccustomed armpits and elbows.

Waving a nervous hand, the steward called, 'Julia Felix, bring us some cakes!'

Plates of honey cakes were already set out for their mistress to hand round. ' 'Scuse me for bein' so slow, ladies an' gentlemen – me old pins is a bit shaky!' she joked, trying to put them at their ease. Oppio trotted round with wine cups that Victoria filled at a side table.

The steward told his three familiar jokes, the servants laughed obligingly, and as soon as possible they all slid off the couches and bowed to their mistress. 'Lady, we thank you for your hospitality, fulfilling the traditions of this happy occasion. A cheer for the mistress!' They cheered heartily and retreated with relief to their own sitting room, where their real festival dinner was ready.

'Poor souls!' Giggling, Julia Felix collapsed into a chair. 'So embarrassed! There will be a cold meal under the cloths there, Victoria, if you please!'

Victoria dished out lettuce, broiled sardines and the spicy sauces the old lady liked. Oppio, as a free man, stayed with them for this meal instead of eating with the servants. He ate rather shyly, carefully copying the way they handled their knives and spoons. Few women reclined at meals – they all sat comfortably on chairs, where they could reach the table easily; and Julia Felix insisted that Oppio had a couple of glasses of wine, with less water than usual. Gradually, the lad relaxed.

'Miss Victoria,' he asked eventually, 'why can't Mum marry Smarandax?'

'Because he's a slave and Mira is free. Free men or women can't legally marry slaves.'

The boy frowned. 'So they can't never get wed?'

'Not unless I free him.'

'Or she might sell herself to Victoria as a slave too,' Julia Felix said. 'But that would make you a slave with her, as you're not a man yet.'

'She'd not do that!' Oppio was alarmed. He thought for a minute, scratching his nose, squinting worse than usual. 'But that means they can't, not never. So won't you free him?'

Julia Felix snorted a laugh. 'He cost money, boy! To be freed, he'd have to pay a fee of ten per cent of his value – or Victoria would. How much would that be, girl?'

Victoria shrugged. 'Prices are down, with the flood of slaves coming in from Judaea. But for a trained steward – five hundred sesterces at least.'

'So, er, fifty sesterces to pay.' Oppio whistled.

Julia Felix nodded. 'Yes, a lot, boy! You could buy a little slave girl for twenty. And if he was free, Victoria would have to replace him—'

'No, she wouldn't.' Oppio was definite. 'I heard 'em talking. He'd stay; he says you're ben— er, benevolent an' considerate an' he'd never find a better place.'

'Don't blush, girl!' Julia Felix chortled; Victoria blew a raspberry in response, despite what Caenis had said.

Oppio was too serious to smile. 'An' Mum don't like not bein' married to him, special now wi' the baby comin'.' Victoria puffed slightly; she hadn't known. But what should she expect? 'An' he wants to marry her, see? An' if he was free he could, an' everybody'd be happy.'

'Well!' Julia Felix eyed him quizzically. 'Who put you up to this, eh? Your mother?'

'No, lady!' Oppio appeared indignant. 'Just me an' Celia was thinkin'. An' Celia said, could I ask? She'd never have the nerve, not since the fire – scared o' her shadow even. It ain't fair that some folks can do what they likes an' others can't.'

'Fair? Huh!' The old lady snorted. 'You expect the world to be fair? You are free, and whole, and healthy – is that fair to those who are slaves, or ill or crippled? Or to your little sister, afraid to face the world? Life is not fair. Nowhere, at no time. Complain to the gods. Accept it, or go mad fretting about it.'

Victoria raised a hand. 'No – well, not entirely, Julia Felix. We can try to make it a little better. At home in Britain, slaves are seldom ill-treated because, at the gods' whim, you may suddenly be a slave beside them, or even be their slave instead. Fairness usually returns to you. Cruelty always does. Which do you want to spread?' She tilted her head to stare at Oppio. 'They want to get married? And they'd really stay with me afterwards? Smarandax is a good steward, and I like and respect

92

your mother — and you and Celia too. I'd not like to lose any of you. You — you're like my own family.'

She paid no attention to Julia Felix's sniff of amusement, but studied Oppio's face carefully, astonished not at how much he felt this, but at how deeply she responded to it. 'I was a slave for a while and I hated it, even though it was by my own choice. I can understand . . .' Sly little snippets, Oppio and Celia, planning to bring this up when the old lady was there as a witness! Or maybe it was his own idea. Not a nasty one, of course, he was a good lad. Like pleasant, capable Mira, and timid Celia, and fidgety Smarandax, all of them good people . . .

A new thought came to her. If she was caught in her plotting, then her slave Smarandax would be tortured to procure evidence against her, and probably Mira and Oppio and Celia too. Like Petronius, she must give them the chance to get away, without the threat of being seized and crucified as runaways — as well as all the other problems they would have.

Firmly, she nodded. 'I'll free Smarandax, when we get back to Rome. But let's keep it a secret, as a surprise for him!'

'Ooh, yes, lady!' Oppio's ugly little face was alight. His plan had worked! 'Oh, you're wonderful! Thank you!'

What a great feeling, to give joy! Victoria smiled sweetly at Julia Felix's exasperated shake of the head.

'Emotional nonsense!' the old lady told her. 'It'll be the death of you some day!'

'No, it won't,' Victoria assured her. 'I'll always fight. Always.'

Julia Felix tutted. 'Of course, girl. But that may not be enough . . . What's that racket? Ah, some of the youth club come to visit. They think they can sing, poor souls. But their girls are always good entertainers. Is it Drusus dressed as Father Saturn as usual?'

'Who else? He's the biggest,' Victoria commented. 'The red gown suits him, but he's well away already, look at his ivy wreath just hanging on one ear, and he's got wine stains all down his false beard!'

Julia Felix tutted. 'Oppio, fill up all the cups, and we'll drink to a merry Saturnalia and a happy and prosperous new year – and may all our wishes come true!'

VII

In early January Victoria returned to Rome, to be welcomed by her full household of servants and gladiatrixes. Oppio leapt down in the yard already boasting, 'Mum, Mum, I drove just about all the way! Miss Victoria says as I'm near as good as she is, an' she give me a knife for the Saturnalia! I'm a man now, I'm her groom an' gettin' paid a proper wage! Great, eh? Hi, Celia! Can't stop to gossip, gotta stop bouncin' about an' get on.' Mira smiled at Victoria over his preoccupied head as he bustled to see to the ponies, waving casually to his shy sister – half hidden in the shadows behind the door, but clearly excited or she would never have appeared at all.

Victoria thrilled with a simple pleasure at their cheerfulness. When had she felt like this before? Not since . . . not since playing with her little sisters in Londinium.

The builders were finished, Smarandax reported happily. 'That Miss Africa, mistress, oh my, what a wonder at keeping them working, dry or rain! What a tongue, oh yes – and what a wallop if they didn't do a good job, or were disrespectful, even to me! And, er, when they started missing days, because they were working on another house, she found their other

95

site and put such a scare into them they came here every day, didn't dare not!'

Proudly, he showed Victoria the niche by the front door where the statuettes of the household gods and the gladiatrixes' favourite deities, Mars, Fortuna and Isis, were installed. 'We put them in early, mistress, and they get their incense every day, oh, yes. The yard walls are done, and Mira says the kitchen is splendid. And, er, the roofs are all watertight and the bathhouse is fine, er, since we got the furnace flues right – Miss Africa kept them at it eight days solid till it worked, oh didn't she just! And the new well gives plenty of water for it. Only we, er, we didn't know if you wanted frescoes.'

'Oh, certainly. We'll be entertaining editors and people hiring gladiators – we must look prosperous. Yes, find us painters, Smarandax. We'll have the traditional combat scenes, but with gladiatrixes.' Victoria smiled to herself. No hesitation there; her head was clear and hard again. Maybe it was her bad leg that had been poisoning her mind into soft weakness. She was glad to be over it; soft got you killed.

Africa was equally positive. 'I've bought in the new weapons we need, Victrix, real and wooden training ones. Tyrannia was stabbed in a brawl over a man during the Saturnalia, but everyone else is back, and we have two good new volunteers. And a man gave us a mad slave, told me to get her killed off, he didn't want the bother of having her legally executed.'

'Mad?' Victoria asked in some alarm.

'Don't worry,' Africa soothed her. 'He threw her baby out to die when its crying annoyed him, and she attacked him. But I've talked to her. She'll never go in the arena, but she's a grand cook and Mira needs the help – Celia's not enough.'

'Um.' Victoria nodded acceptance. 'Give her a new name. If he ever asks about her, we'll tell him she died in a training accident.'

'We've all been helping with the work, carrying stone, cutting wood, mixing concrete. Good for us, strengthened our muscles. We enjoyed it – eh, girls?'

The gladiatrixes milling round them groaned and jeered.

'Ruined my hands – I'll never do fine embroidery again!'

'When did you ever, you daft prawn?'

Africa smiled, smug as a cat. 'The training gear's being erected tomorrow, same as in Pompeii, and then we'll get the yard tramped hard and cemented. Even with the new kitchen and bathhouse, we've got about sixty paces by ninety for training – plenty of room.'

'Will you join us for training, boss?' Chloris asked.

'Of course!' Victoria assured her. 'My leg's getting stronger every day.'

'Fit for the arena?' They all looked hopeful; she felt warmed by their concern.

'Soon. And if I don't keep an eye on Africa, she may let the standards slip.'

'Me?' Africa snorted mocking contempt. 'You must be as stupid as you look!'

Victoria dived for her; they wrestled for a minute until Victoria took advantage of Africa's consideration of the bad leg, tripped and threw her. She stood over Africa, grinning to hide the pain in her thigh, shouting her war-cry in triumph.

Africa thumbed her nose up at her, laughing. 'Learn from that!' she instructed the cheering, laughing audience. 'Never underestimate an opponent, even one who seems hurt!'

On the sixth day of January, to Victoria's astonishment an eight-bearer curtained litter entered the yard, with ten lictors as escort. A senior Roman magistrate; it couldn't be to arrest her, they'd send soldiers for that. Did he want to hire gladiatrixes for a set of games?

While the Amazons greeted the lictors and the big, strong bearers with enthusiasm as a welcome break from boring training, Caenis climbed from the litter, slim and lithe despite her age and the enveloping wrap that turned her into a cocoon of peach and cream. She caught Victoria's hands and, smiling, drew her forward to meet a sturdy, elderly man in a toga with a broad purple edge. 'You're not going to slip away this time, my dear! Sabinus, this is my friend Victoria Aegypta, whom I know you have admired in the arena. I'd have introduced you before, but she was too shy. Victoria, Flavius Sabinus is Vespasian's older brother. He's Urban Prefect yet again this year, poor man, trying to keep food flowing into the city and troublemakers off the streets. What a thankless and hopeless task!'

Sabinus must think Caenis was crazy, calling any gladiatrix shy, especially one with bright British clothes and tattooed scalp! And Victoria had dealt with a queen and an emperor; a mere magistrate, even the man who ran Rome, wasn't going to overawe her. 'Honoured to meet you, sir,' she said to the jutting jaw and eyebrows and the weary, pouched eyes.

Sabinus bowed rather stiffly. 'I understand that the honour is mine. Considering your fame. And your efforts for my brother. I appreciate the risks you run.' His tight-lipped mouth softened in an unexpectedly charming smile. 'Vespasian will be grateful. As I am. I thank you, on his behalf. You will be heartily rewarded.'

Victoria had to return the smile. 'Thank you, sir—' She broke off.

A small fair-haired man in a beautifully-braided, expensive, black tunic was extricating himself from the litter, his back towards her, leaning on a silver-trimmed ebony staff. 'You know Galba Cramus, Victoria,' Caenis introduced him.

Galba – the Emperor's freedman? And Cramus . . . ?

He turned. Yes, she knew him. Cram.

Victoria was appalled. 'He knows? He'll betray us!' Her hand went to her sword.

Caenis seized her wrist. 'No, he's with us! He'll help bring Galba down! Would I risk everything? Trust me, trust my judgement! Come inside, in private, and I'll tell you!'

As Smarandax and Mira brought hot wine and cakes to the

small, neat reception room and added charcoal to the burner, Victoria eyed her cousin distrustfully. Yes, he'd want to destroy any emperor — but never to help build up another one. Would his enthusiasm for destruction not damage what she and Caenis and old Julia Felix had been building so cautiously over the past months? Victoria made herself smile slightly: control, don't show your thoughts. She'd keep a careful eye on what he did — and what she said in front of him.

Like Victoria, Cram's smile did not reach his cold eyes, but his words were warm. 'I swear to you, Victoria, I'll do all I can to assist you. Emperor Galba likes my playing, and people forget that musicians have ears. I was, as you'll appreciate, keeping mine open for word of you, and when I heard you were a friend of Antonia Caenis, who is close to Vespasian, well, I thought for a while — you remember telling me to do that? And chatted to soldiers on leave . . . I more or less knew what I was looking for, so it wasn't too hard to find out what you were doing. Since I decided that I approved, I made myself known to your friends, offering to help. As you said yourself, a whisper in the right ear can influence a decision. Not too often, of course, or they'll become suspicious, but even if they do . . .' He held his right hand over the brazier as sign of good faith, and his voice resonated in the bard's trick Victoria recognised from years ago in Britain. 'May all the gods of Britain and of Rome witness that I solemnly swear, my right hand in the flame, by my hope of crossing the bridge of swords to feast for ever with my father and the heroes in the Land of Gold, by my love and duty to Boudicca, that I will never betray you, any of you, to Galba. Will that satisfy you, Victoria?'

Reluctantly, Victoria nodded. 'Of course, Cram! I know you'd never break an oath like that!' However, she could not force herself to look enthusiastic. He was smart as a squirrel; he'd find a way to wriggle round the oath if he wanted to, and she was sure he did – or would later. But she couldn't say so. Get down to business, to cover her misgivings. 'Could you persuade Galba to adopt Otho instead of Piso?'

'Otho? No!' Sabinus broke in abruptly.

She blinked. 'Not Otho? But—'

'No.' Sabinus's voice was dry. 'If Otho is adopted, Piso will feel insulted. Also afraid that Otho will see him as a possible challenger, a future threat, and assassinate him. Piso will feel he has to act. He is a plain, honest, down-to-earth man, so we shall have open civil war. His senatorial friends and their clients will be fighting the Praetorians in the streets of Rome. Hundreds dead, whoever wins.'

Unseen behind him, Cram was smirking; that thought pleased him.

It didn't please Sabinus whose face was grim. 'No. We want Galba to adopt Piso, simply because Otho will not allow it. He's as ambitious and far more ruthless. He loved Poppaea, but divorced her without any argument when Nero decided to marry her.'

'Wise man!' Caenis interjected, caustically.

'Yes. He was well rewarded for that, made Governor of Lusitania. Now he wants his reward for helping Galba to the throne. He expects to be made his heir. He is deep in debt, needs to be able to dip into the Treasury to pay his creditors. If thwarted, he will strike. He knows everyone expects Galba to fall soon.'

Cram grinned. 'You've heard what happened? As High Priest, Galba was making the New Year sacrifice for good fortune for himself and Rome when his laurel wreath fell off, and while he snatched at it the sacrificial cock wriggled free and flew away!' He flapped his arms like wings and crowed, looking remarkably like a cockerel.

Stern-faced, Sabinus nodded. 'Two shocking omens of disaster – I hope for him alone, not for all Rome.' Only Victoria noticed the narrowing of Cram's eyes. 'But Otho is a much more subtle operator than Piso. What is more, he hates the idea of civil war. He will do nothing openly. He will pretend to accept it. But as soon as he has organised everything, he will have Galba killed. Piso as well, maybe. I hope not. But that will be only two deaths, instead of hundreds. And another greedy rogue on the throne, ready to be toppled by a better man with the army behind him.'

Caenis nodded. 'Not fair and straightforward, Victoria, not clean, not honest – but the best in the end for Rome.'

Sabinus agreed. 'We cannot allow respect for what is right to prevent us doing what is best.'

'I'll do all in my power to assist you, sir,' Cram said, sincerely.

Victoria rubbed her scar uneasily and shrugged. This was hypocrisy and cheating – but if they all thought it would work . . . Politics . . . And her cousin was lying – or no, not exactly that; but at least he had plans of his own. What was in his mind?

A few days later, in the Praetorian camp, Galba announced his heir: Piso. Since he did not offer any payment to the soldiers, to encourage them to accept the young man, he and Piso left the camp in a strained silence.

As Sabinus had prophesied, Otho showed only amused resignation. 'No, no! I've no ambition to become emperor!' he jovially reassured Galba. 'I wish this worthy young man all success! Give me Africa or Hispania to govern next year and make my fortune, and meantime I'll enjoy my children's company, and make speeches in the Senate in your praise!'

Cram, however, reported that Otho collected a bribe of a million sesterces from one of Galba's slaves for persuading the Emperor to grant him a plum job, and the next night entertained the Praetorian Prefect to dinner. 'What did they discuss, eh? The price he'll pay for the throne?'

On the fourteenth day of January, a fine, cold day after much rain, Victoria told Smarandax to put on his best tunic; she wanted his help with some official business. They arrived in the Forum about noon. Most of the senators were out, strolling among the stalls and statues that cluttered the cramped, crowded Forum, discussing the latest news. The legions in Germania had refused to swear loyalty, and had acclaimed their general, Galba's old pal Vitellius, as their new Emperor; another revolt, to add to the unease in the city.

Otho was there, beaming and bulky in his purple-edged toga among a huddle of friends and clients, climbing into his litter. However, it was jammed in the crowd. He jumped out again, losing a sandal – a bad omen – and hesitated, but then hurried off east towards the Praetorian barracks.

Victoria led Smarandax to join the queue of people waiting to see Sabinus. The chief magistrate was sitting under a canopy to deal with pleas and reports in public as usual. Not a man to worry about appearances, he was wearing long, thick woolly socks and a warm shawl wrapped round his head and neck over his toga, against the chilly wind.

When they finally stood before him, he greeted them formally. 'Victoria Aegypta, how may I help you?'

'Flavius Sabinus, Urban Prefect, I wish to emancipate my slave Smarandax here, in thanks for faithful service in a time of great difficulty for me.' She grinned at Smarandax as he gasped.

Sabinus disapproved. All very well to free a slave in your will, or after a lifetime's service when he was too old to work, or if he could buy himself free, or even for an act of great devotion like risking his life to save yours; to do it for such a petty reason was deplorable, setting a bad example to other slaves – they'd all expect to be freed next! However, as a favour he had agreed that he would officiate at the ceremony, which would normally be conducted by one of the minor clerks at tables behind him. He nodded reluctant permission. 'You have the document of manumission?'

'Here, sir,' Beside her, Smarandax was shivering, panting with shock and excitement. Victoria smiled down at him. 'Bear up, man! Don't you want to be free?'

The document was soon inspected and stamped, and the fee paid. Victoria handed the little scroll to Smarandax. 'Don't lose that, now!'

'Oh, mistress! Oh, mistress!' he whispered, his bony Adam's apple jumping as he swallowed nervously.

'Not mistress now, Smarandax. Lady, yes, if you'll stay with me—'.

'Of course, lady, of course!'

She smiled and slapped his arm. 'Good. Then here – the final thing.' She handed him the simple, bag-shaped woollen cap that no slave might wear; the cap of liberty.

From his raised platform, Sabinus nodded down. 'Put it on, Victorianus Smarandax, freedman!'

Smarandax's hands were trembling as he pulled it over his dark hair. 'Oh, lady! Thank you, lady, thank you, lady can I ever—'

Suddenly people were shoving into the Forum, shouting,

'The Praetorians have proclaimed Otho Emperor!'

The senators scurried up the steps of the Senate House, to shelter there, or away towards their homes and safety.

Hiding his excitement, Sabinus rose and gestured to his lictors to carry his canopy and ivory stool indoors. 'Everyone remain calm!' he called. 'This may be only a rumour.' His clerks packed up fast and ran for the Treasury offices in the basement of the Temple of Saturn.

Victoria drew Smarandax up the steps to the Temple of Vesta to watch what happened. 'Is it true?' he whispered. 'Is Otho truly in rebellion?'

Bright-eyed, she shrugged. She hoped so.

Shortly, Galba, Piso and their clients hurried into the Forum from the Domus Aurea to investigate. Galba, purple-faced with the fluster, his toga bundled on all awry, was angry, confused and afraid, grunting. 'Is it true? What's happened? Doesn't anybody know?'

Only seconds later, a dozen mounted Praetorians shoved ruthlessly through the crowd towards them, shouting, 'The rebels are beaten!'

Galba's clients cheered, but Victoria shook her head; something felt wrong.

'I killed Otho!' one of the soldiers bellowed.

Still puffing after his hobbling rush, Galba demanded imperiously, 'On whose authority? You have no right to kill a senator without your Emperor's command!'

The man spurred forward, grinning. 'Oh, that's all right. We've got the command from our Emperor, Emperor!' He whipped out his sword and stabbed downwards, twice, fast. More Praetorians joined in, striking Piso as well, jeering at Galba's terrified clients and lictors, who fled through the ring of spectators.

The killers jumped down and triumphantly hacked off the corpses' heads. 'Otho'll give us plenty for these, eh lads?' One tried to pick Galba's up by the hair, and cursed when he found it was a wig. He wrapped the bald head in a strip cut from Galba's toga, remounted, and led the cavalcade galloping back towards their barracks.

The Roman crowd were always an avid audience of public events. Unthreatened, uninvolved, they parted to let the soldiers ride away, and flowed back to stare in fascination at the corpses. Some cheered; some wept; some laughed nervously.

Sabinus, responsible for order in the streets, exchanged the briefest of glances across the Forum with Victoria before sending his lictors to lift trestles from a flower stall. 'Carry Piso's body to his home, and lay Galba's in the Temple of the Caesars. Respectfully! He was your Emperor!' Then he turned to the crowd. 'Go home. It is over for now. Go home. The new Emperor will make his own announcements when he is ready.' Sighing, he walked back into the agitation of the Senate House.

No great tension, no tragedy, no squalid, pathetic drama as there had been with Nero's death. A few seconds of shouting, a flash of steel, a heavy man falling slowly, hidden by horses — and it was done. Even the crowd's reaction felt flat.

Smarandax, shivering beside Victoria, voiced her own thoughts. 'Emperors should die more — more impressively.'

'Yes. It feels so petty. But after only — what — six months? And after all he's done — does he deserve more? Ach, come on, free man.' Shaking herself free of melancholy, Victoria slapped Smarandax's shoulder. 'Home.'

This was exactly what they had planned. Wasn't it?

That evening, Otho told the assembled Senate that the Praetorians had dragged him off the street and forced him to undertake the rule of the Empire, to amend the injustice and tyranny of Galba's reign. Purely for the sake of Rome, and to avoid civil war, which he begged them to believe he feared above everything else, he had reluctantly acquiesced.

The Senate, Sabinus among them, applauded and swore loyalty to him. They had little choice; the chamber was lined with Praetorians.

Victoria sighed. How long would Otho last? After all, another acclaimed Emperor, Vitellius, was already marching south from Germania to challenge him.

And Vespasian was waiting patiently in Judaea for the right moment.

She hoped it came soon.

VIII

In March, Victoria, whose leg by now was almost fully fit, was summoned to the Praetorian barracks. Every lanista in Rome was in the courtyard. 'What's up?' she asked.

Her friends shrugged. 'Don't know. Vitellius's Rhine legions walloped Otho's army up north last month,' one offered. 'They're saying if one legion in Hispania could make an emperor, seven in Germania can do it better.'

'Vitellius is a fat, greasy slimeball,' someone muttered, 'but he's got seven legions, an' damned good generals.'

'Otho sent messengers to him early on,' another declared. 'He offered to make him second in the Empire, and was flabbergasted when Vitellius replied, "I lead the largest army. You should give way to me." ' Eyes rolled, faces grimaced all round the room.

'Otho's prayin' an' sacrificin' so hard there ain't a white bull left in Italy. Must be plannin' sacred games now, old-style, to please the gods wi' men's blood.' They nodded, soberly cheerful; that was good tradition. And good business.

However, when the Praetorian Prefect appeared, their orders were surprising. 'Emperor Otho is hiring all your fighters. Every one. No, not for games.' The Prefect was a new man, the fourth in six months since Tigellinus, Nero's commander and spymaster, had been lucky enough to be allowed to retire. The last Prefect had been so unpopular he had been murdered by his men after only six days. This one drew a deep, defiant breath, looking – could it be? – embarrassed. 'We are raising new legions, conscripting every man of an age to bear arms. Emperor Otho has commanded that a legion be formed from gladiators.'

'Us?' A roar of disbelief. 'We're not soldiers! By Mars, we don't take orders—'

'By Mars, you do!' the Prefect snarled. 'You're trained fighters – so fight for your Emperor! Army pay, and a bonus of fifty sesterces a man when we wallop the rebels!'

To encourage them, he poured out a sackful of the new sesterces Otho had had struck to celebrate his accession, with the optimistic motto PAX ORBIS TERRARUM – Universal Peace. They did not inspire the lanistas; one spat, carefully not quite onto the coins. The Prefect had to shout over the tumult. 'Muster on the Campus Martius the third day from now, fully armed – and not wooden swords, either! Any gladiator who doesn't appear will be executed as a traitor.' He glared round. 'So will his lanista.'

Into the sudden hostile silence, someone asked, 'Novices too?' That started a babble of questions. 'What about food? Tents? Cooking? Can we take our own slaves? And mules? Who'll repay us if our slave gladiators are killed? Who's responsible if they run? What is army pay? Eh? You expect gladiators to fight for that?'

'They have their choice!' the officer snarled. 'Fight or die!'

Victoria slipped out quietly. The Amazons weren't going to like this!

They didn't. They nearly mutinied. It wasn't until she pointed out gently, 'If you don't turn up I'll be crucified alongside you,' that the hubbub simmered down. However, once they accepted that the imperial order must be obeyed, they settled to planning.

'We'll look after ourselves, nobody else will. Our own cooking pots and tents, the small mule-cart. No, Oppio, you can't come, I'll drive. Blankets, boots, thick socks, warm clothes for the mountains. Sensible clothes, Africa!' Victoria grinned at her friend's exaggerated dismay. 'No parade gear; fighting armour and weapons only. I said no, Oppio!'

Even though they were all rushed off their feet, and the omens for the next day were less good than for the planned one, Smarandax and Mira insisted on bringing forward their wedding so that their friends could attend. In the nearest suitable temple, a small room with no statues, only a faded painting of Juno and Vesta on the back wall, Oppio proudly led his mother forward. Mira wore her red wedding gown, which she had saved from the great fire as the most precious thing she owned, and a hired headdress with its traditional seven bands of tightly-rolled wool. The teenage priest competently sacrificed two doves, inspected the entrails and declared that the goddesses were pleased to witness and bless the marriage. Almost paralysed with nervousness – at his shoulder as groom's witness, Victoria feared she would actually have to support him – Smarandax took Mira's hand and together they sprinkled the wine, wheat, incense and oil, and made their vows. Fighting her shyness, Celia threw flowers in their path as, waving branches of laurel and singing bawdy songs – Mira giggled, Smarandax blushed – the Amazons escorted them home, where Smarandax presented Mira with the symbolic key to his room.

Mira and the new cook had prepared a fine feast of pies and pickled fish, and eight amphoras of wine, each as big as Oppio, to celebrate both the wedding and the traditional gladiator's farewell party; it might be their last, and they made the most of it.

Next morning, the Amazons swayed rather unsteadily on to the Campus Martius, near the river just outside the walls of Rome.

To demonstrate their independence and their annoyance at being conscripted, two thousand gladiators were milling about, drinking, rough-housing, arguing, singing, fighting cocks and dogs, ignoring or mocking orders from a frustrated quartermaster.

A cohort of regular legionaries eventually had to be brought in to split them into approximate centuries. Each century got a mule-cart and driver. Gradually the carts were loaded with their equipment, and each century was marched – well, urged in an untidy huddle – off to learn how to erect their tents and get supper.

The Amazons wandered round the nearby market stalls to buy snacks and useful items like spare bootlaces and lucky charms, joked and gambled with acquaintances, mischievously added to the confusion. As Victoria had expected, they were dealt with last. By the time the quartermaster got round to them, the only cart available was a rickety wreck, with decrepit mules and a toothless ancient for a driver. One cooking pot with a hole in it, a two-legged tripod and a single tattered strip of canvas were their camp kitchen and tents.

'We have our own, tribune, already set up down at the far end. We're used to travelling. We just want food from you.' Victoria smiled in sweet sarcasm at the weary officer. 'You do have that?' Fortunately for her, considering the officer's frazzled temper, his clerks still had plenty; they always planned to sell leftovers. Her insistence and Africa's charm got the Amazons their full ration of onions and oil, corn, salt fish and beans, and even an extra amphora of rough wine.

When Victoria visited to Caenis's atrium that evening, she found Cram and Sabinus there with Domitian, Vespasian's younger son, tall and exquisite in wonderfully cut and curled hair and a dazzling toga, graciously condescending – pure honey, except for an irritated moment when he had to look up to Victoria.

'I came in to see who we want to win this battle,' she told them. 'Or doesn't it matter? Both Otho and Vitellius are incompetent, as far as I can see.'

'And you can decide?' Domitian acted admiration. Overacted. 'Such far-reaching influence! Astounding!'

Victoria avoided Cram's sardonic eye, which clearly asked if the father of this patronising playboy was really who she wanted as emperor. 'Only reaching so far, sir. I doubt, frankly, if I could make Otho win. His new legions are conscripts hauled from their farms or shops, mostly too old or too young, and almost untrained. But I can make absolutely certain that he loses.'

'Really? Do tell me – tell us – how?' Over-sweet; he thought she was too stupid to notice the underlying contempt.

Relishing Caenis's delicately cynical smile and Sabinus's growing anger, Victoria spoke flatly. 'I have some influence among the soldiers, and more among the gladiators. I can't speak out openly, Otho would have me executed for treason, but I can make them feel we have no chance, wonder why we're fighting for a pinch of salt. I can maybe even make them turn and run before the battle.'

'I could help you there,' Cram suggested. 'Properly sung, a song can do exactly the opposite of what its words seem to say. I'll come with you.'

'No!' She smiled, to soften her sharp, instinctive refusal. 'Better if you stay with the Emperor. And his officers. Twist their minds towards failure, as you did with Nero.'

Domitian's eyebrows rose. 'You, Cramus? You affected Nero? Oh, awesome! You must play for me some day at a dinner, to demonstrate your mastery. Though my friends are senators, ex-governors and generals, much stronger personalities than Nero, so you mustn't feel bad if you have less success with us.'

Unexpectedly, Victoria's hackles rose in defence of her cousin's skills. 'Your friends will be impressed, sir. Maybe even yourself.'

'Oh, I'm sure I shall!' Domitian flashed his excellent teeth at her, but the smile did not reach his eyes; she wondered if it ever did. 'As I'm certain that your sneaky-spreading of false rumours will be terribly effective. Not what I'd care to do personally, but for a gladiatrix – and British – er—'

'Domitian, these people are risking their lives for your father. Treat them with courtesy.' Sabinus's voice was heavy with displeasure.

'But I'm trying to!' the young man protested, all innocence. 'I swear I am!'

Cram's eyes caught Victoria's, for one instant full of amusement, as so often in Britain. Momentarily, they were again allies in face of this arrogant, insulting snob – she could read his thoughts as, she was sure, he could read hers. Then his face and lips tightened again.

Caenis, blandly peace-making, said, 'I don't think it matters which wins, Victoria, as long as the legions all feel they're fighting for trash. Can you spread that feeling?'

'Yes, I can do that.' She'd try to keep the Amazons safe, too. Battlefields were dangerous places.

But if Domitian's eyes were to be believed, this was a battlefield too. He disliked Caenis, and her, and Cram, and Sabinus, and would do them an ill turn if he safely could, despite what they were doing for his father. Thank Bouda, Vespasian had an older son; she'd not lift a finger to help this one.

Lazy, spendthrift Otho, who loathed civil war, faced it bravely. To show his men how tough he was, he marched on foot with them, unshaven, till his feet were too blistered to walk. They laughed at his useless bravado, the few older, experienced men.

Even before they met, the decurion appointed to officer the Amazons resented the humiliation of having to deal with women. They reacted to his open scorn by acting as he clearly expected; they confused right and left, gossiped constantly, wandered off, complained, wailed when he hit them or shouted at them, offered kisses and invitations to him and every man they met. Frustrated and furious, he vanished after the second day. Victoria was left in charge.

On the other hand, Oppio — trust a boy — turned up at noon on the first day of the march. 'Didn't expect me to stay behind, lady, did you? Not when you needs me.' He was right; the army driver had dropped out an hour after they started, coughing helplessly in the dust raised by the carts in front.

'Oh, Bouda! I told you no! I'll wallop you tonight, see if I don't!' But that evening she preferred to forget it, for truthfully she was glad of him. He took over most of the driving and the care of the mules and the little cart from Nero's stables, which somehow had never been returned.

Suetonius, whom Victoria remembered without fondness from Boudicca's rebellion, was Otho's extremely competent general, and marshalled the new legions to win a couple of skirmishes against Vitellius's men. Victoria carefully kept the Amazons on the fringes of the fighting. When they complained, she told them, 'I've been in a battle, you haven't. Believe me, you don't want to, either. I don't care if people say we're shirking. It's not like the arena. It's worse. There's no profit in getting killed out here. Trust me – I'll see you right!'

She insisted on carrying all their gear with them, even onto the battlefield. 'You go hungry and cold if you like, but I want food and a tent on hand!' The girls grumbled at the extra work, but were glad of it after the first battle, when it was a full day before the legion's carts caught up and the rest of the army got anything to eat. The little cart came in useful, too, for collecting armour they stripped from the dead, a sickening job even for those used to the slaughters of the arena, which rapidly convinced Victoria's friends that she was right about staying as far out of the fighting as possible. Soon all the Amazons, even the retiarii, had complete body armour, though they complained that it squashed them, and they all preferred their full-face arena helmets.

'You look almost like real soldiers!' Victoria told them. They groaned and jeered.

After the minor successes, Suetonius advised Otho to wait. The legions from Moesia were coming to support him. Also, Vitellius was still away up in Gaul, and his general here, Valens, was excellent; if they could delay until Vitellius, a less competent strategist, arrived to take charge, they would gain an advantage.

However, Cram whispered in the Emperor's ear that maybe the Moesian legions would support Vitellius instead, and Victoria's delicate campaign of dissatisfaction persuaded many men to desert. Otho could not stand the uneasy tension. He must get it all over, one way or the other. In camp near Cremona, he insisted on an immediate battle.

Suetonius gritted his teeth and chose his field of battle carefully. He ranged Otho's hotchpotch army before dawn along the first solid bank above the wide, meandering River Po, to catch Vitellius's advancing army at a disadvantage. The centurions stood behind to give orders, keep the men fighting, kill anyone who turned to flee.

Slowly, the darkness lightened. The mist turned grey and then white, a layer of gleaming pearl above the water. Battle trumpets and drums approached. Most of the fighting was concentrated on the bridge to Cremona, but here at the edge one of Vitellius's experienced legions, toughened by fighting through the forests of Germania, advanced steadily, slowly, wading chest-deep through the warm water and mud.

Today, Victoria was the person right at the end of Otho's troops. Naturally, the gladiators had been posted on the far left of the army, the place of least honour, and the gladiatrixes on their left again. They had a good defensive position, among a line of scrubby bushes on top of a steep, soft, head-high bank cut by the winding river.

Behind the Amazons an olive orchard sloped gently down, with bushes straggling among the small, gnarled trees. About a hundred paces behind them, a little copse of five ancient trees with some bushes and brambles, apparently too sparse and scanty to hide anything, gave surprisingly good cover to their cart. The mules had been hobbled and tethered among the trees to graze, while Oppio tied branches on the sides and top of the cart as camouflage.

Victoria peered through the scrub to check; no, the cart couldn't be seen easily unless you knew it was there. 'If we have to run, everybody throw these ten-ton shields into the enemy's faces to knock them back down the cliff here, and race for the cart to hide before they climb up here and see where we are.'

'You think we'll have to?' Chloris asked, rubbing gooseflesh on her arms.

119

'Only the gods can see the future – and I sometimes wonder about them!' Victoria joked. But yes, she did think it; she hoped for it. At least, she thought she did.

'Oof!' Africa hefted her chin-to-knee army shield. 'Heavy as a broken heart. I'd prefer my net.'

'Lighter, but less useful in a battle.' Clenching her teeth to stop herself being sick with tension, Victoria grinned back. 'Is everybody happy? Is anybody happy?'

Behind them, Parmenia defiantly snapped, 'Yes!'

'Lucky you! I'm scared.' Africa had fought too often to need to pretend. 'Worse than the arena, this. Colder.' She yawned with nerves, shivered, and hid it with a joke. 'Specially at this cursed time of the morning! I should still be in bed. No parade, and the band's lousy. There's no – no glamour.'

'And no big prizes!' Victoria had been mentioning that occasionally ever since they started out, murmuring complaints or over-cheerful confidence, sneering too much at the northern legions, subtly discouraging everyone.

'Listen! Look there!' Chloris called, pointing over Victoria's shoulder.

Heavy splodging and splashing. A twinkle of steel. A gilded eagle standard, apparently floating on the layer of mist. A line of filthy knees emerged under it, lumbering up out of the water. Above them coalesced bright-painted shields, dripping kilts, cursing helmets.

'Get ready!' Victoria called. Waste of breath – everyone was already stiffening, gripping weapons, raising shields. She swallowed, wiped her sweaty palm and drew her sword. Oh, Bouda, keep us all safe this day! Should she run, try to start a panic?

Twenty paces away, still knee-deep, Vitellius's men halted and poised their javelins.

One of the champions of the arena suddenly yelled, 'Mars take this! I'm not a snotty soldier!' He whirled, bulled through the line behind him, cut down a centurion who tried to stop him, and ran. Victoria almost laughed. Almost.

His example slashed like a scythe in hay among the other gladiators, and on through Otho's new, raw legions. When Vitellius's javelins ripped the sky, half Otho's army was already fleeing.

Unused to fighting at a distance, some of the Amazons turned to watch the running men. Africa laughed: 'I prefer men to follow me, but this time maybe we should—'

A javelin drove behind Chloris's shield, below her breastplate, deep into her side. She screamed and tugged at it, gasping with pain.

Vitellius's men were floundering forward, charging up out of the clinging ooze.

'Parmenia, Romana, take her back, we'll hold them!' Victoria yelled. The men on their right had already gone. 'Half a minute, girls! Bouda help us!'

Romana yanked out the spear-point. Big Parmenia simply

121

picked Chloris up and ran with her for the cart.

Knocking aside swords, stabbing desperately down between their weighty, unfamiliar shields, Victoria and the rest of the Amazons faced the soldiers scrabbling up the little cliff. Eight of them took wounds in those few seconds, but they downed four men, whose fall hampered others. 'Shields! Run!' Victoria yelled. They hurled their heavy shields down into the faces of the attackers, broke away and fled. Victoria kicked the face of the front man still clambering up and toppled him backward, before she followed her friends ducking through the bushes. Gods, her leg was still too weak for rough ground . . . Stop thinking, stupid! Run!

No-one chased them, thank Bouda. The nearest centurion was bellowing, 'Hold the line there, you poxy donkeys! Stop at the top! Women? You got women on the brain, you poxy billygoat! Don't care if it were poxy Venus herself, stand here! The poxy cavalry's coming, they'll mop up!'

'Listen, hooves! Get down!' Victoria hissed. Oppio had already tripped the mules, wrapped their heads in cloaks to make them lie quiet, and laid branches over them. The women crouched under the cart and among the bushes, weapons ready for a last desperate, hopeless defence if necessary. 'Gorgo, bind up that ankle and stop cursing, it's not your Achilles tendon, it won't lame you! Anybody else badly hurt? Good! Oppio, get under the cart — yes now! Everybody still! Quiet!'

Chloris strangled her moans. Victoria took her hand. 'Brave, brave!'

Silently, praying to all their gods, the twenty women watched three thousand of Vitellius's horsemen, who had come far round on their left to outflank Otho's army, charge slashing and cheering into the fleeing gladiators and soldiers – past and away towards Cremona.

At the top of the bank, Vitellius's infantry paused briefly to wring out their tunics, collected their thrown javelins, reformed their lines, turned left and marched smartly past and away towards Cremona.

Soon, Victoria sat up cautiously, taking what felt like her first breath in a year. 'All gone, I think. Oppio, up a tree and keep your eyes open. Chloris, we can see to you now.'

Teeth clenched, Chloris lifted the hand she was pressing over her wound.

They knew about wounds; this one was mortal. Chloris's gut had been punctured, and possibly her liver. She would die slowly, over maybe ten days, in terrible pain.

There was only one thing to do: a quick, clean death.

Chloris nodded to them, smiling tightly, wordlessly accepting her fate. She gripped Victoria's hand and hauled herself up to her knees, grasping Victoria's leg to steady herself in the traditional posture of the defeated gladiator. 'My honour to know you all. Keep your shields up. See what happens if you don't!'

One of the novices sobbed. Romana put an arm round her.

Africa snarled at them both. 'Don't disgrace yourselves and us, you stupid cows! We take the steel with courage. The dead are free!'

Chloris called out something in Greek, then said firmly, 'Now!'

At Victoria's swift, expert thrust, Chloris collapsed bonelessly. 'Cross the Styx proudly, Chloris, in courage and freedom, with the love and respect of us, your sisters.'

After a long moment, Africa slapped Victoria's arm. 'Wake up! Time to go!'

Victoria drew a long breath through her nose, nodded grimly, and wiped her sword. 'No mourning. The dead are free. Stop snivelling, Oppio. Peritana, you should know better, you've seen people die before. Get the mules up and harnessed. Move, people! What are we waiting for? A cup of wine and a picnic?'

Chloris was laid out respectfully, with coins in her mouth to pay Charon. 'No, we'll not bury nor burn her,' Victoria decided. 'We haven't time and it would draw attention. Cover her with those branches. Romana, you were her best friend, you take her bangles, yes, do! Wear them to remember her; no reason why looters from the town should have them. Right, let's go. Behind the cavalry, before their infantry; we should be all right if we keep a good watch, ready to run for cover if we see the horses coming back. Oppio, a steady trot, and try to avoid running over bodies, it upsets the mules.' And her. She was really getting too soft to survive!

Soon they caught up with the scraps of the routed army, scattered and desperate after dodging the cavalry. They were mostly too young or too old, torn from their homes and families by Otho's frantic conscription, plodding, stumbling, staggering along, grim or blank-eyed or sobbing, now facing execution as traitors if Vitellius caught them. Only drawn swords stopped the cart being seized. It was soon laden with the wounded; nobody argued when Victoria tossed out the tents and much of their gear to make more room.

She felt sick. The arena was a fair combat – facing death, but with the cheers of the crowd to hearten you, and a better than even chance of surviving if you fought well. Battle brought the chance for gallant comradeship, amid death, mutilation, pain, blood. She had seen the Iceni joyously head-hunting at Camulodunum, and suffered in the other side of it – the destruction of Londinium. But this – this was worse than anything she had experienced. Defeat was terror, heartbreak, despair; atrocious, even if you'd worked hard to bring it about.

She thought back to the sacred command laid on her. Destroy Rome? Well, she had seen off three Emperors already. Not bad, for a plain lass from the far side of beyond.

It would bring a better time in the future. She just wished she felt good about it now.

IX

Against all her expectations, Victoria actually enjoyed quite a lot of the next six months.

The Amazons got back to Rome before most of the army but behind the news, which had been carried by fleeing cavalrymen, and also behind a troop of Vitellius's cavalry who came ahead of the main army, rode unopposed into the city and took over the Senate House and the Domus Aurea.

Victoria led the troupe home silently, slipping into their house after dark without any fuss. 'Quiet, Celia, don't cry! Yes, I'm glad to see you too, peachblossom, and you, Mira. Oppio, see to the mules right away, poor beasts, they've done well by us. So have you — you'll drive for the Blues yet! No trouble, Smarandax? Good. Now, everybody listen! We were armed as men, so we can hope that's how we were seen. So, we've been here quietly all this time. Otho forgot us, or else didn't want us, we're only women — all right, all right, I'm glad you have enough energy to groan! Don't announce it, that would draw attention, but if anybody asks, that's what we say. The other gladiators won't be talking to Vitellius, not if they can help it, and he can't chase up everybody. With any luck nobody noticed we were away; and if they did, they may not inform on us; and if they do, Vitellius may not bother with us since we're back.'

And for whatever reason, he didn't.

Cram, when she next heard from him, was safe, playing his lyre and singing in the Domus Aurea as before. He reported that Otho had killed himself quietly and decently when he heard about the rout; he had been emperor for ninety-five days.

Valens, Vitellius's general, arrived with the main army. Several senators who had opposed Vitellius too strongly were executed. To Victoria's glee, Valens replaced the Praetorian and Spanish bodyguard with his German auxiliaries. In a strange country, speaking only the little Latin they had learnt from their centurions – mostly army commands and curses – he felt they would cling to their Emperor, their comrades and their legion, which was now their clan, and were less likely to be persuaded or bribed into disloyalty.

They did create problems, however, though not for him. Whenever they felt bored, or lonely for their forests and homes – which was most of the time – the Germans went carousing through the streets in huge smelly furs and feet – they thought bathing was unnatural and unhealthy – beating up anyone whose face displeased them. Several houses and many shops were looted; no-one was punished. People stayed indoors with their shutters closed, as Rome nervously awaited its latest emperor.

Caenis told Victoria, 'I've closed my shop altogether for the time being. Poor Sabinus! If he had any hair left, he'd tear it!'

Victoria grinned. 'I've been making friends. It's not something you can do, but they like me and the girls!'

The very first group that she had met were arguing with a wine-seller, voices rising, long hair and heavy bearskin capes bristling as they gestured, on the point of gutting him.

Victoria called out in Iceni, 'Hey, men! Wait a minute!' Some might have travelled enough to learn a few words of a dialect near enough her tribe's language to understand her.

She was lucky. One of the Germans swung round, astonished. 'You not Roman!'

'I'm from Britain. Iceni. Wait a minute, now.' She turned to Latin, speaking fast to the barman while the Germans eyed her scalp and clothes. 'Idiot! Barbarians, yes, but they're not stupid. They know you're over-charging. See those swords? They're not just ornaments, they could cut you in half – vertically. And do you think their officers would even scold them? Wake up! Say that was the price for all of them, not just one, and in future charge the proper price and look happy. You'll still make a fair profit, they'll come back again with their friends, so you'll have plenty of custom, and your left side won't be waving goodbye to your right! A good deal, eh?'

The stall-keeper agreed.

The interpreter bought Victoria a drink and introduced

himself and the others. 'I Helmann – he Boioric . . . Kernac . . . Ethelrix.' Their names jumbled in the crowd, their grins were wide and cheerful under their plaited moustaches. One said something to Helmann, who nodded and turned to Victoria. 'You meet us girls? Big friend girls?'

She grinned. 'I can take you to meet twenty strapping-big girls, mostly very friendly. But you'll have to be polite, or they'll beat you up!' They laughed uproariously.

Unlike Romans, the Germans were accustomed to woman warriors. The Amazons loved them, trained and partied with them, stopped street traders from cheating them, and introduced them both to the Baths, which after much suspicion they decided were sissy but fun, and to Rome's passion, chariot-racing, which they adored.

That put Victoria in mind of something she had planned to do.

One fine July dawn, she told Oppio, 'Get my chariot, sprat. I'm going to the Circus Maximus. The Blues are training there today, and I want to see old Balbus.'

'The Blues? Wow!' Naturally, Oppio knew all about them. 'They're the best team, far better than the Greens, and the Whites and Reds are rubbish. They've got the best drivers and horses, everybody bets on them! And Balbus, he's the finest trainer ever, he knows more about horses than horses do!'

She chuckled. 'Not hard, lad. Horses are as daft as sparrows.'

His eyes squinted even worse than usual in shock at the insult to his beloved ponies. He made a hideous face at her, before begging, 'Can I come in with you, lady? See the drivers and horses, maybe even see Chrixus – he's the champion! Please?'

'No, no, you wouldn't enjoy it. Don't look at me in that tone of voice! All right, all right, if you insist! Tell you what; we'll drive right in, onto the course. They set up a little driving course to teach the youngsters and the young horses how to manoeuvre. If there's nobody working on it, I'll ask if you can have a go.'

His face lit up like a full moon. 'Could I? Will you? Really? Ooh, wow!' He didn't stop talking about the Blues, not for one whole minute, all the way to the stadium.

Fifty chariots were training there, cantering round the long Circus Maximus course, amply wide for six four-horse chariots abreast. The vast stands that could hold almost a quarter of a million people were empty except for some idle watchers and keen fans, or spies for opposing teams. Though the cheaper and women's seats high at the back were wooden, the lower banks of the seating recently destroyed in the great fire had been replaced in stone, like the imperial boxes beside the finish line. Above the walls of the narrow spina in the centre, three hundred paces long, the big carved balls and dolphins which were moved to mark the number of laps still to run were richly gilded, for in Rome racing was even more important than gladiatorial games. Even emperors might envy the wealth of champion drivers.

In the open space before the high entrance gates at one end of the track, Oppio was soon weaving Victoria's little chariot in and out through the training ring of empty barrels, at a shy trot at first, but then with more confidence at a slow canter, showing off to a critical audience of grooms, while Victoria stood talking to the head trainer, Balbus. 'Thunder and Lightning are nippy, but he's the one got them so supple and responsive. Not bad, eh?'

His face deliberately scornful, Balbus studied the boy. 'S'pose I've seen worse. He ever driven a race?'

'Scarcely. My horses are trained for twists and turns in a tight arena, not seven-lap marathons. He's not too young?'

'Neh.' Balbus sucked his yellow teeth. 'We get six-year-olds beggin' t'muck out an' run wi' buckets, hopin' t'work up t'drivers. Yah! Lookit that!' A barrel went flying. He spat noisily, pretending contempt. But the lad had promise . . . 'He got the guts f'r it? If he ain't, he's worse 'n useless, he'll get hisself killed, an' horses as well, as is more important.'

Victoria nodded. 'I know racing's dangerous, like the arena. Crashes, accidents . . . But at least the drivers aren't trying to kill each other.'

'You think? I c'd tell you stories . . .' Balbus snorted. 'I'll think about it. Talk t'me trainers, see if we got a team bad enough f'r a novice t'learn on. Come back in a month.'

'Balbus, you know every one of your hundreds of horses! Why not now? He's keen to join the biggest and best team in Rome, rather than the Greens, or even the Reds or Whites. They're not as good, but he's desperate just to drive, so if you put him off . . .'

'Whites? Monkeys on fleabag donkeys!' Balbus spat again. Though rumour had him rich enough to buy the Circus Maximus, he despised fancy manners, and always acted like the roughest of yokels straight off the farm. However, the warning had its effect. He abruptly yelled to a passing driver, 'Paulus, bring 'em here. Steady! Don't haul on 'em like a sailor or you'll get your flappy hands on a stick for bumwipers! Oy, you lad! Oppio, is it? 'Op it, then, over 'ere!' He jerked his head. 'Right, take 'em twice round.'

'Me? Them? Here? Now?' The challenge to drive a racing chariot in front of his heroes shocked Oppio to breathlessness.

'You, them, here, now,' Victoria confirmed, taking her ponies' reins from him. 'I've seen you racing along the back roads.'

Oppio glanced up briefly, twitched a desperate, one-sided grin, puffed, stepped cautiously into the light racing shell, clicked his tongue, shook the reins – and nearly fell out as the horses leapt forward to join their circling fellows. Grabbing the wickerwork side, he just managed to stay on his feet. Victoria gritted her teeth; the horses were running ragged, not together. Oppio was being carried, not driving.

Near the far turn, though, the lad realised the inside horse was going ahead, shoving the chariot away from the wall. He singled out the reins and slowed it, to bring them all round level and tight. Balbus grunted. 'Huh! 'Bout time he got a grip on 'em!'

Taking a grip on himself, feeling the team's growing steadiness, Oppio urged them on for a second lap, faster, with much more control, even overtaking a few of the other teams.

When he drew up beside Balbus and Victoria, panting and flushed, he was pleased by Victoria's smile; but it was Balbus's grudging nod that sent his heart racing like the horses. 'Seen worse. F'r a first time. But I din't tell ye to race 'em. You listen t'me in future or I'll skin yer.' The old man grunted deep in his throat, and nodded again. 'In the stables to muck out every day afore dawn, same's other lads. A'noons, we'll see about drivin'. Maybe.'

Oppio's face glowed delight. 'Oh, sir, lady – th-thank you! How can I . . . but I'll always . . . I'll never, never . . . I'll pay you back my apprentice fee . . . I'll—'

'Not till you're famous and rich!' Victoria scolded him affectionately. 'Now we'll leave Balbus to get on with his work. Thank you, sir – he'll do us both proud!'

From then on, she saw Oppio as seldom as Celia. He practically lived at the Blues' stables on the northern edge of the Campus Martius, and when he did come home was so tired he could barely speak. Mira, however, assured her that he was ecstatically happy. When the other boys beat him up for being the boss's pet, he took the bruises and the loss of a front tooth as proof of his skill and status. His mother scolded him about his language in the house, learnt from Balbus and the stable hands. Even Victoria learnt some energetic words she'd never heard on the palaestra.

In early August, when the new Emperor finally arrived, Victoria organised good seats for her German friends for Vitellius's Coronation Games.

She fought in them for the first time since her operation; not in her chariot, as her leg was not quite firm enough yet to balance, bent-kneed, in the bouncing cockleshell, but on foot, in her normal fighting style as a Thracian, with a small shield and her short sword, her right arm armoured. She beat Artemisia – an experienced gladiatrix from Capua who had beaten her once before – after a long, messy tussle, for the woman knew some tricks that Victoria only avoided more by luck than skill. In the end, though, Artemisia weakened with loss of blood, and although the Vestal Virgins granted her mercy she died under the surgeons' hands. Victoria felt the usual regret, but no more, and some relief that here in the arena at least her new, unwelcome soppiness didn't weaken her.

Helmann and the Germans cheered wildly, brandishing their swords, to the alarm of nearby spectators and the amusement of those safely at a distance, and added bellows of their own to Victoria's war-cry of triumph. Considering their fierce loyalty to the Emperor, in case they understood her she changed her yell to a simple 'Victory!'

She liked the big, long-haired men; they reminded her of her uncle back in Britain. They liked her, too, at least enough for her to be able to distract them on occasion from robbery and murder, which added to her popularity with the Romans.

On his way south with a swarm of hangers-on and toadies, Vitellius had been feasting at the expense of the towns he passed through and then looting them, kidnapping their young women and men as slaves, generally making merry — well, making himself merry. In the Domus Aurea he continued this wild extravagance, spending and giving and wasting, gifts and games and feasting. To pay for it, he increased taxes, sold the rights to tax the richest provinces of the Empire even if those rights had already been sold to others, sold powerful positions and legal decisions, raided temples for their treasures, seized nine-tenths of the estate of every freedman who died, demanded 'loans' which everyone knew would never be repaid. Anyone who complained was killed, with less compunction or legality even than Otho or Galba had shown. The violence and looting increased. Sabinus was in a fury of frustration, for his vigiles were beaten up if they tried to stop the disturbances.

Caenis came in secret to the palaestra in late August, walking from the city with only Lucius as escort. Her usually

135

immaculate hair was untidy, the dark dye washed out of its spreading wings of grey, and she wore a shabby gown and cloak. Called by the porter when the persistent old woman would not go away, Smarandax nearly refused her entry – till he recognised her icy stare. He hurried to usher her to a shady seat in the garden, sent Celia for wine and warm water to wash the visitor's face and feet, and called Victoria in from training.

'Yes, thank you, Smarandax, another cup. Oh, beautifully cool! Hail, Victoria!'

As Victoria came in, puffing, to wipe her face and hands with a damp cloth, Smarandax poured her a cup too, waved out Celia with the basin and towels, and bowed himself away.

Caenis gripped Victoria's hand with a grin of triumph, her usual aplomb swamped by excitement. 'Victoria, I had to come. A letter from Vespasian at last! He's been wounded twice, didn't want to tell me till he'd recovered, in case I worried – I worry more when there's no news, but that's men for you. But he paraded his troops last month to swear loyalty to Vitellius, as he'd done for Galba and then Otho, but this time they refused! They just stood and stared at him, in silence. And next day when he came out of his tent, they hailed him as emperor! They knew what he was planning, of course, soldiers always do, and they agree, they've forced his hand. He can't go back from that! He has to go on now!'

Victoria felt her heart clench. 'Oh, Caenis, it's happening! It's really going to happen! After all this time – I can scarcely believe it—'

'Everybody's agreed to support him! In Antioch, Mucianus, the Governor of Syria, told his soldiers they were being replaced by the German legions and sent north. They didn't fancy that, so they've all sworn to Vespasian, and the Egyptian Governor ordered his legions to do the same. All the legions in Moesia, led by the Third you spoke to in Syria, they've all sworn loyalty to him as well, all on their own. Ten legions altogether. Most of the local subject kings are backing him, offering their armies too, and apparently Berenice, the sister of King Herod Agrippa in Judaea, is madly in love with Titus! Or at least he is with her. She's ten years older than he is, almost forty, but incredibly lovely, Vespasian says.'

'You'll be glad it's Titus she has her eye on!' Victoria chuckled at Caenis's fervent nod.

'Indeed! Vespasian has told Mucianus to lead the eastern legions to Rome across Greece, but they'll take weeks, so Antonius Primus, one of the legates in Moesia, is dashing with the Danube legions straight for Rome. They should be entering Italy any day now.'

'Oh, it's happening, it's happening!' Victoria chortled. 'And I've news for you, too. Helmann, my pet German, says there's another revolt up in Germania, it's getting as rambunctious as Judaea. Vitellius can't draw any more men from the north. So he's going to have to face Vespasian's men with only what he has round here. The gods are with us!'

'Yes.' Caenis's beaming smile faded. 'But there is a problem.' She sighed, suddenly looking every day of her nearly sixty years. 'Sabinus and I have advised Domitian to leave Rome, but he dislikes me so much, and he's so popular among the senators' wives and daughters, that he'll not go. I'm afraid Vitellius may take him as a hostage.'

'Or you,' Victoria suggested.

'Me? I've no importance—'

'Are you crazy, Caenis? Is there a soul in Rome doesn't know how Vespasian values you?'

Caenis laughed, wryly. 'Or how little he would turn aside for me? Step aside from a throne, for the sake of an old freedwoman? He'd be the only man in the world who'd do that! Don't be silly.'

Victoria eyed her friend shrewdly. 'But, for you, he is the only man in the world. And you're the only woman for him. More even than beautiful Berenice! She'd not go for the boy if the man was available. Proof, if you need it, that it's you he loves.'

To Victoria's amusement, Caenis actually blushed. 'I'd not let him give up for me, anyway. But no, I'm in no danger, less than Sabinus. But Vespasian's son, that could be different. Domitian disagrees, of course. He says Vitellius would never harm him, it would be dishonourable, and anyway he can look after himself. Stupid boy. Twice over.'

138

Victoria grinned at her friend's return to dry humour. 'I could kidnap him?' In her private opinion, though, if Vitellius killed off that supercilious snotter, Domitian, it would be the best thing that could happen for all of them.

'And send him off to his father? Oh, how tempting! But not really practical. I don't know where Vespasian will be. He didn't say, in case of spies and assassins. But I think he's planning to hold back the grain supply ships in Egypt to create a shortage in Rome, so make sure you have plenty stored. Then when he finally arrives, with the ships, he'll be welcomed. Meantime, Sabinus will try to persuade Vitellius that more civil war would destroy Rome, hoping that if he sees big armies coming against him, and food riots here, he might give in, resign instead of fighting.' Caenis sighed again. 'Oh, I hope so! But I doubt it. I do doubt it. The senators are still mostly on his side, for all I can do, they're so stiff-necked! They don't want a mere provincial nobody like Vespasian, however honest and competent he is – and not a few of them just because he really is honest and competent!'

'Snooty, snobby scumbags,' Victoria commented. Caenis tutted at her language, but did not disagree.

The troubles in Rome grew worse and worse. The homesick, protected Germans grew more and more destructive. When the legions were ordered north to throw back Primus, everyone sighed with relief.

The gladiators were again conscripted into the army, as Vitellius desperately scraped up more men. The Amazons were not called on. Cram reported, 'Vitellius blames you women for causing the rout among Otho's men. Though he was delighted last time, he says you're unlucky, doesn't want to risk it happening to him.'

It made no difference. In October, Primus attacked Vitellius's army at exactly the same place where it had attacked Otho's men. A second time, even without Victoria, the gladiators ran away. Vitellius's army, like Otho's before it, was defeated.

Unlike the last time, though, Cremona was destroyed. Utterly. Looted and burnt, and every soul inside slaughtered; and not by Vitellius, the debt-ridden, gluttonous, decadent villain Victoria was trying to depose, but by Primus, the general and agent of her chosen emperor, Vespasian.

Victoria sighed for the little town, with its bright awnings over the wineshops where she had joked with her friends such a short time ago. She wondered grimly whether Vespasian would be disgusted and shocked, or whether he had ordered it as an awful example to Rome: 'Surrender or this is what will happen to you!'

'No, he'd never do that!' Caenis insisted. 'But – well, now it's done, he might judge that the devastation of a small town was worth it, to save Rome later.'

'You mean Primus did it on his own because he's a

murderous brute, but Vespasian will accept the slaughter and not condemn him?'

Caenis sighed and nodded. 'Not in public, at least.'

Politics was a dirty business, Victoria thought. 'I hope it's worth it all.'

Caenis gripped Victoria's hands. 'It will be, my dear. It will be!'

Vitellius's last two Italian legions were sent north to hold back the advancing army. At Narnia, they drew up on the road facing Primus and his men. The commanders conferred between the armies for ten minutes; then, as Primus led his soldiers forward, Vitellius's men drew off in good order to the sides of the road, waited while Vespasian's legions marched through, and fell peacefully in at the rear.

The combined army advanced to within two days' march of Rome, and stopped, waiting for Vitellius to act: come out and fight, flee, or resign. Remember Cremona . . .

That afternoon, Caenis sent Lucius running with a message direct to Victoria: 'The mistress calls you to come at once, miss. Flavius Sabinus has done it! Persuaded Vitellius to resign! The Emperor has gone to announce his decision to the Senate! She says to say you've done it!'

X

Every road out of Rome was choked with refugees fleeing the invading army. Rich and poor, some hurrying unencumbered, most laden with huge bundles, shoving wheelbarrows, riding donkeys and horses or on foot, in litters carried by sweating slaves or crowded carts pulled by belligerent mules or vexed oxen, all who could were leaving. The rich headed for country houses or friends in quieter parts of Italy; the poor just headed away. The road west to the port of Ostia, naturally, was worst of all.

A chariot driven by a single woman with a boy as escort was eyed covetously by the frantic fugitives. Luckily, Victoria was easily recognised, and stayed standing, not kneeling, to be more visible. Her obvious, stalwart readiness to fight, and the sword in clear view at her belt, saved them several times from being attacked.

It took over two difficult, frustrating hours to work through the crowds to reach the city. 'I'd be quicker walking!' Victoria huffed to Lucius. However, near the Porta Lavernalis the flood of people suddenly stopped, and they could trot forward along an empty road.

At the gateway they discovered the reason.

Rome was being fortified against Primus's approaching army. The ancient walls and gates were being hastily repaired and strengthened, and soldiers stationed only a couple of arm's lengths apart all along the top of the wall.

Though all the other gates were closed from sunset till three hours before dawn, when farm carts trundled into the city markets, merchants needed access to the Tiber's wharves and warehouses through the Lavernalis and Trigemina Gates at all hours. These gates had not moved for years. Their wood was rotted and their metal hinges corroded solid. Now they too were being fortified; across the roadway, between the huge stone gateposts of the Porta Lavernalis, a troop of Germans was building a barricade of overturned carts, stone and beams tumbled from nearby buildings. Bonfires were being lit as evening fell.

Some of Victoria's friends were there, and hauled back a cart to let Lucius lead her ponies past. 'You sure you want in, Victrix? In now, you stay long time, maybe, till Primus run away!' Boioric called.

Clearly he had not heard that Vitellius was resigning, and he might be infuriated by the news. After all, what would happen to the unpopular Germans when their protector left? Better be cautious than show off her information. 'Don't worry, I'll walk home if I have to!' Victoria called, and drove on.

Worming through the agitated crowds, eventually they reached a small secluded courtyard which Oppio had discovered months before, a safe place with a gate and a sheltering tree to leave Thunder and Lightning. While Lucius tied the ponies' blankets over them, as it was cold and beginning to rain, Victoria gave the yard's owner five sesterces: 'Rub them down, Justus, get them oats and water, they may be staying here for a while.' Then she and Lucius hurried up the hill in the dusk.

There was shouting over towards the Forum. Celebrations at the news of Vitellius's abdication? Or rioters – or Praetorians – killing Germans?

Caenis's porter peered through the peephole at her knock before opening: 'Madam is on the terrace, miss.' He was nervous, and the slaves in the kitchen area were making far more noise than usual. Natural excitement, she thought. They had done it. Done it . . .

Caenis was craning forward over the balustrade, peering out round the corner of her house to see the Temple of Jupiter, its gilded roof glowing in the last of the sunlight high above the Forum. Victoria grinned. 'Careful you don't go over, your brains will do better in your head than splattered across the street down there. Caenis, you're white as a toga, what's the matter?'

Caenis seemed to find it hard to speak. 'You haven't heard?'

'Heard what?' Victoria's heart pounded. What had happened? Was Vespasian dead?

'Vitellius, the flittery two-faced slime-hearted scoundrel!

He made his farewell speech to the Senate, and they urged him to stay, but he refused; Sabinus kept him steady. But then he started out to go north to surrender to Primus, and his litter couldn't get out of the city. All the gates were shut, and his Germans all thought he was there to encourage them, and cheered him. He was too scared of their reaction to tell them he was leaving. So he went back to the Domus Aurea, where Sabinus and all our friends had gathered to celebrate, and declared he'd stay on and fight! And when Sabinus argued, he ordered the lictors to arrest him! Sabinus and Domitian had to fight their way out of the palace. They fled to the Temple of Jupiter – it's a sanctuary, anyone inside is supposed to be safe – but Vitellius has ordered the Germans to break in and kill them. It's – it's disaster!'

Victoria drew a long, hard breath. 'Only for the people in the temple. Vespasian is still coming, and you and I, we can't give up, so close. We can't!' Sabinus would be missed. She didn't care about Domitian.

Caenis, though, felt differently. 'Victoria, will you go and see what's happening? Maybe you can do something. Sabinus and Domitian – Vespasian's own brother and son – please try to save them! I know it's a terrible risk, but I have to ask – to beg you!'

Victoria could not refuse her friend's plea. What could she say? 'I don't much care for Domitian'? No. She shrugged. 'You risked your life for me once. Yes, I'll go.'

Caenis held her back as she headed for the door. 'No, you must disguise yourself! Have you your wig? No, of course not, why should you? But a cloak – Lucius! Lucius, find Victoria a long, hooded cloak and a tunic, a man's tunic.'

Victoria pulled the knee-length tunic on over her own bright shirt and wolfskin jerkin – for extra warmth without her trousers – but her legs felt naked and draughty; with a shiver, she put the trousers on again, rolling them high above the knee so they'd not show. That was better. If they slipped down in the dark nobody would notice. She hoped.

'Good luck!' Caenis called after her. Victoria shivered. Nothing brought a gladiator worse fortune than that! But Caenis wouldn't know. She touched her sword blade to avert the evil omen, and hurried through the rain towards the noise in the Forum.

Crowds of men were spectating from a safe distance all round the Capitol, thronging the open Forum itself, the steps of the Senate House and the speakers' platforms, the pediments of surrounding buildings and statues to watch the show. Victoria jostled forward through the mob.

Since there were no windows through which the Germans could break into the temple, they had hauled down a statue, carried it up the Capitoline Steps to the pillared portico, and were using it as a battering ram against the gilded bronze doors. Hammering from the rear told of a side entrance being assaulted, while yet more soldiers were jumping across the roofs of the lesser temples and halls alongside.

Vespasian's supporters were clambering about on the temple roof, ripping off the gilded tiles and hurling them down onto the heads of the attackers. By the light of bonfires of wood broken from the snack stalls round the Forum, and firebrands arching up through the dark, the Germans were throwing spears and axes up at the defenders. A cheer rose as a spear pierced a man lit by the flames. He toppled back inside.

Some Germans raised a ladder from the roof of a basilica built against the temple wall, and a stream of them climbed up to battle with the men on the temple roof. Someone slipped and fell, screaming briefly amid a clatter of tiles. Other soldiers jumped down within. Shouts and screams began to echo from the holes in the roof.

Soon, the doors were swung open from inside. Howling in triumph the Germans swarmed in, to drag out about a dozen prisoners.

The officer in charge stepped forward, raising his baton for silence. The spectators surged forward to hear him, up the flight of steps and round the sides of the platform under the temple portico. Victoria felt it was safe enough to go with them, though she took care to stay at the back of the crowd, among the pillars, and keep her hood up.

'Conspirators!' the tribune shouted. 'Against Emperor Vitellius and Rome!'

The crowd roared hatred at the prisoners. Among them was Sabinus, his toga gone, his tunic bloodstained and torn. He had worked for years to run Rome well, but now the people he had served screeched for his death, and cheered maniacally as the officer drew his sword, gestured to his men to force Sabinus to his knees, and chopped off his head. The body was thrown down the steps, where the crowd jeered, spat and kicked at it.

There was nothing Victoria could do. Nothing anyone could do.

Where was Domitian? Not among the prisoners, none of them was tall enough. Dead inside? She almost hoped so . . . No. She must do what she could.

Some of the mob were going into the temple, to gawp round. Among them, knees bent to disguise her height, she filtered in through the door and slipped back behind it to study the scene.

The vast hall was black dark, the only light from the broken roof, one triple lamp on the high altar and some torches held by a few Germans hauling bodies towards the door. Shadows danced crazily over bloodstains, shattered tiles, discarded clothing and wrecked furniture.

Victoria's foot caught in a bundle of discarded togas tucked in behind the huge door. She glanced down as she freed herself. It twitched.

A quick glance round – nobody looking her way – she

knelt beside the bundle, hissed, 'Keep quiet!' and lifted a corner to reveal the person huddled below.

Domitian's wide eyes reflected stray gleams of torchlight. Even in his fear, he was venomous. 'You! Helping your German friends?'

'Ssh! Helping save your life!' she hissed.

He snorted, almost silently. 'Save me? How? How can I get out past all these stinking savages?'

It wasn't the time to argue about who was a savage. 'Pretend to be dead? No, they're stabbing the bodies, just to make sure.'

'Not a good idea.' Recovering slightly, he was sneering.

'Well, we'd better find some way, or you're for a quick trip across the Styx,' Victoria snapped. 'Like your uncle. I'm sorry about that.'

'Sabinus? They killed him? Without trial?'

'You heard the cheering? Rome seems to be all for Vitellius.'

'No, I recognised a lot of them. This mob is all clients of the senators, sent out to riot on Vitellius's behalf. Not the same thing.' Political comment helped calm the young man.

'Some of them have come in like me. Quite a number. Can we disguise you, to join them? No, you can't have my cloak, I need it to hide my head. You *would* have to be so tall! And wearing a bright-yellow tunic, so noticeable! But . . .' Victoria weighed the toga in one hand. 'This is a long length of cloth – what can we make of it? Wrap you like a woman? No respectable woman would be out tonight, though, and you'd never pass for a pleasure girl. You're pretty, but not that pretty.'

Someone shoved the door back, knocking the carving against her head. She froze – no, they'd not been noticed – and rubbed the bump. The smoothness of her scalp and the mental picture of a girl melded oddly in her mind.

She drew her knife. 'Bend your head this way. I'm going to shave off your hair. Don't argue, we haven't time. You Romans are so proud of your hair, they'll never dream you'd go bald to escape. Stop squirming or I'll cut your ear off. Look, idiot, you choose; lose your hair or your head!' Ignoring the young nobleman's affronted glare and muttered curses, she kept shaving.

Typical of Roman opportunism, dozens of citizens had wandered in to nose about, poking into corners they had never been allowed near before, offering the Germans drinks and bites of sausage, nipping bits of gilding and ivory off the statues and memorials, dodging soldiers who tried to order them out. Soon, they found amongst them a priest of Isis. If his long white kilt and yellow sash, and the shawl draped round his shoulders, were stained and slightly ragged-edged, in the darkness no-one noticed.

Domitian's rather unevenly scraped head gleamed acceptably in the patchy torchlight, and soot lined his eyes in the dramatic Egyptian style. He paused by the piled bodies, chanting in gobbledegook as he edged towards the door. The incense he carried sizzling on a gilded platter was actually his own perfumed curls, fed strand by strand into the flame of a candle stump on a fallen tile, but the stink produced a vague atmosphere of foreign holiness.

Behind him Victoria, alert for any trouble, stiffened. That man at the door was one of Tigellinus's old spies – and another one over there, studying the people milling round the temple. They might recognise Domitian's height. Bouda, what should she do?

A diversion. Preferably one that wouldn't draw attention to herself.

At Domitian's shoulder she murmured, 'Spies at the door, checking for traitors. Don't go out yet. I'll make a disturbance. Wait for it. Then just walk out. Don't run. Go to your father's house, to Caenis.'

He almost froze, but had enough control to keep chanting. One thing Roman education taught was self-discipline.

She strolled away, knees still bent. Among other curious observers she wandered towards the marble altar at the rear of the temple. The stink of blood hung round it from centuries of sacrifices. Above it towered the latest huge statues of gilded, ivory-inlaid wood, of Jupiter Optimus Maximus, his wife Juno and his daughter Minerva. Behind were ranked older statues of these and other gods, some ancient, cracked and worn, but all the more awesome and venerated. In one corner stood The sacred chariot Nero had driven to Caenis's house. Above, the wall's were layered thick with wooden plaques and shields, ancient offerings to the gods. To either side finely-carved seats, tables and cupboards lay tumbled in the fighting. The floor was littered with broken tiles and cloth and other debris from the battle, including the half-burnt remains of some of the torches, which had been tossed in and hastily stamped out.

On the altar flickered a single oil lamp, somehow surviving the fighting around it . . .

A fire . . . ?

Victoria's heart clenched. She had suffered in two great fires already. The first had driven her from Britain, and set her on her course to fulfill the commands of her gods and her Queen; the second had taught her what really needed to be done in Rome. A third – oh, no!

But a third might complete the gods' design. Three was the sacred number.

Fire . . . Yet again . . . And here, destroying the house of the greatest of Rome's gods . . .

She shuddered in fear. But what other way was there?

Clenching her teeth, pretending casualness, she lifted a torch, relit it at the lamp, dropped it on a handful of smashed candles inside a broken cedar-wood cupboard to hide the flame, and forced herself not to flee, to drift quietly towards the door, praying with all her soul, 'Bouda, you have protected me in the arena until now. I beg you, protect me from the gods of Rome!'

She was about ten steps from the doorway when a shout rose from the rear of the temple. 'Fire! Fire! Let me out!' In front of her, Domitian was swept past the watchers in the instant

152

panic-stricken rush of people, safely out into the darkness.

Heart racing with triumph and worry – he might still be caught, she must overtake him, protect him in the dark streets – she joined in the rush, forgetting to keep her knees bent . . .

'Stop that one there!' The officer and a dozen Germans jumped forward, swords poised. She stopped perforce. Poised to fight, she glanced round – a priest of Isis, standing praying over Sabinus's body, brusquely turned away and walked off down the steps, unnoticed in the crowd. Good, Domitian had that much sense – though she knew he'd not have stopped to help her even if he could.

She clawed for her sword and dived aside, to go down under a pile of big Germans.

'Yes, that's the conspirator! Pull off the hood and you'll see.'

She cursed as she lost her sword, but went on kicking, wrestling with all her strength, every trick she knew. In vain. They were too many, too heavy, too strong.

Behind their grunts and curses, over the thump of blows, she heard the voice again. 'Don't kill her, the Emperor wants her! Stun her, you fools!'

Before Victoria was fully awake again, the guards hauled her to her feet and shoved her staggering forward among the other prisoners, her wrists tied tightly behind her. She clung to her swimming senses. If she fell, they'd just drag her. Down past Sabinus's body and through the mob they were hustled, among curses, spittle, stones and blows rained on them. More

153

important was a stabbing pain in her left hand, probably a broken finger.

By the time the guards paused to report to the officer at the door into the Domus Aurea, her head was clearing. She realised that the light around her was not only from the clouded moon, nor from the torches of her captors. Behind her, flames were pouring through the roof of the Temple of Jupiter. She felt a vicious satisfaction; the most sacred temple in Rome, after the Temple of Vesta, and she had destroyed it. Even if they killed her, as they were surely going to, she had done that much of her duty, at least!

Victoria was separated from the other prisoners and pushed along the well-known corridors, past exclaiming, staring people. Maybe not as many as there should be? The thought flickered; could the slaves and clients be slipping away, as they had done from Nero? A new set of German guards took over. She knew some of them. They could not help her even if they wanted to, which was unlikely, when she was proved an enemy of their Emperor. At least they didn't hit her. They escorted her – half carried her – through the high gold doors into the main banquet hall, a huge expanse of marble and mosaics filled with ranks of tables and couches, busy with slaves serving wine and the last dishes of a feast.

On a couch at the head of the hall, surrounded by his most important clients, sprawled Vitellius himself. Half drunk, gross and painted like an eighty-year-old Nero, he was bulging out of a tent-like silk tunic of royal purple embroidered with pearls, his gold wreath askew across his forehead, his face and tunic smeared with gravies and the juice of the peaches stewed in honeyed wine that he was munching.

Victoria clenched her jaw to stop herself sobbing as the guards forced her to kneel. Her tunic was ripped, and her shirt beneath it. One of her trouser legs had unrolled itself. Blood was smeared and splattered over her face and clothes from her nose and swollen mouth, where two teeth were loose. She knew she looked ridiculous. Bound, battered, sick, faint, her head and hand and bruises all over stabbing at her, humiliated before the man with most reason in the world to kill her, surrounded by enemies all booing and hissing the traitor so dramatically produced before them – she had never in her life felt so helpless, so despairing.

No!

Never give up, never stop fighting!

Disregard it all! Ignore the dizziness, the nausea, the pains, tie it all away into the black bag. Don't give them satisfaction by collapsing in front of them, as if in fear. We take the steel with courage! The dead are free!

Vitellius raised a hand for silence, pointing a plump, white, many-ringed finger at her in accusation. 'Foul witch! Filthy traitor! You have conspired to destroy the city that has given you everything – fame, wealth—'

'Rome has given me nothing! Nothing except pain and

155

contempt and heartbreak!' Victoria interrupted. 'All the good I've gained, I've paid for twice over!'

'But Rome gave you the chance to get it!' the Emperor snarled. 'And this is how you repay her! Vile conspiracy against your Emperor, raising civil war! We have your colleague in crime!' He gestured.

Victoria's heart clenched as Caenis was thrust forward, rumpled and dishevelled, looking tired and old, but still gamely trying to smile at her friend.

'Oh, yes!' Vitellius gloated. 'We know all about you and your plots to set that oafish old workhorse Vespasian on the throne! Who supports him? Ex-slaves and low-lives!'

'And the army,' Victoria snapped. 'Ten legions—'

At Vitellius's gesture, her German guards knocked her down and hit her with their spear-butts. One landed hard on the scar on her leg, forcing a grunt of pain. 'Lie still, Victrix!' one of the guards hissed, unexpectedly. She peered up, and recognised Helmann. A friend? Not really, he'd not help her – but perhaps he'd not hurt her either, unless he was directly ordered to.

The Emperor was sneering. 'Not all of the army backs your precious Vespasian, as you see, slut! Nor any of the Senate!' The surrounding courtiers cheered. 'Nor even your fellow-conspirators!' He beckoned. 'Meet the man who uncovered your plotting!'

Cram. Of course.

XI

'You called me traitor.' Victoria spat at her cousin in Iceni. 'Who's the real traitor, though?'

'Speak in Latin!' the Emperor commanded.

She flicked a disdainful glance at him. 'Very well. Let everyone hear the truth! This man swore before the gods that he would not betray us—'

'I swore,' Cram interrupted her, smugly, 'I swore not to betray you to Galba! And I did not! Nor to Otho! I kept my oath, twice over! But now I serve Rome's true emperor!' The courtiers applauded. Cram bowed floridly.

'He has told us of your vow to the pagan witch-queen to destroy Rome,' Vitellius announced, 'and how you planned to do so by debasing her, forcing the noblest blood of Rome to bow before a country bumpkin! But he prefers to serve Rome—'

Victoria dragged herself up to her feet again. 'Rome? He wants to destroy Rome far more than I do! I'll tell you who he serves! Why he's betrayed us!' Her voice was still strong enough to pierce the jeering catcalls. 'He's betraying you far more than I am!'

'I am loyal to you, Caesar, before any person alive!' Cram protested.

'That's true,' Victoria spat. 'Your heart's deepest loyalty is to Boudicca, and she's dead! To her and to Britain, not to Rome or anyone here. Not even to me, and you're my cousin.' She glared at Cram. 'Oh, yes, Emperor Vitellius, he wants you to stay emperor – but only because you'll ruin Rome more thoroughly than anyone else could, you great purple hippopotamus! And he wants to stop Vespasian because he'd be a good emperor, he'd run the Empire honestly and well, he's not a greedy, greasy, drunken, fat fart like you!'

She waited for death – if she was lucky . . .

In the sudden appalled silence, leaning on his silver-topped staff, Cram started to laugh. 'Nonsense!' he chuckled. Victoria recognised the bards' trick that made his voice deep and compelling, moving everyone's thoughts rapidly away from her insults before he could be linked with them. 'How could a simple barbarian like myself, all alone, hope to destroy Rome? What incredible rubbish, sire!'

After a long moment's hesitation, Vitellius shook his head. 'Yes, little British barbarian bard, incredible.' Cram bowed his gratitude.

The Emperor shoved himself upright on his couch. 'You, you stupid foul-mouthed bitch, are said to be a good fighter. I intended that you should fight one or two of my German guards, to entertain us.'

'Shall I play for you, sire? To embellish the execution?' Cram reached for the harp slung, as always, at his shoulder.

158

Vitellius considered, rasping his bristly, layered jowls with his hand. 'Later. Perhaps.' He waved a dismissive finger. 'For the moment, I have a different task for you. If these women are traitors to me, then whether or not you are betraying me, you have certainly betrayed them. And I despise traitors.' In a sneering smirk, Vitellius bared his teeth at Cram's sudden apprehension. 'I have a better idea. You may prove your true loyalty to me – to Rome. You will fight your cousin instead.'

The courtiers guffawed at Cram's dismay. 'But I'm not a warrior – I'm a cripple—'

'So is she! And not at her best, is she? Besides' – Vitellius jerked his head to call a slave standing at the rear of the hall – 'we were talking about her after you left. Someone brought me this, that belonged to her. I had planned to let her use it against the long swords and spears of my guards. But you may use it instead, and we'll give her just a knife. That will even things up.'

Cram stared at the object he was offered, as if it would bite him.

Victoria knew it. A sword. A straight blade, rather lighter than legionary swords, with a tiny scene of a boar hunt inlaid in gold. It had been a gift to her in Britain, from Cram's father, her Uncle Arvenic. Her own beloved Needle. Returned to the palace after her last fight, lying forgotten in some store-room, now unearthed by a toadying slave.

Furious, desperate, Cram protested, but received only jeers

159

and laughter from Vitellius and the assembled senators.

Victoria was glad of the argument. It gave time for Helmann to cut her hands free, for her to rub her wrists and hands to ease the stiffness and swelling, and massage her bad leg.

Remembering past kindness, a slave boy risked a beating to bring her a jug of wine. She took a mouthful to rinse the blood from her mouth, and one grateful gulp to settle her nausea. Then, wincing with the pain of her bruised muscles and fingers, she stripped off the torn, bloodstained over-tunic and used a corner to wash her face and head. Yes, she had bumps all over her aching skull, but the sting of the wine on her cuts and grazes revived her considerably.

The boy helped her to fasten her broken finger, the middle one in her left hand, to its neighbours as a makeshift splint, bandaged with strips torn from the tunic. They tied the rest of the cloth tightly round her right arm. Not proper armour, but the best she could do. Her leather jerkin would protect her a little from slashes, though not from a stab; she wished she also had her shield, her helmet, her heavy-buckled arena belt to protect her belly . . . She'd manage without. She'd have to.

Slaves carried the central tables out and packed the couches aside round the room, to clear an area about ten paces long and eight across; not as big a fighting space as an arena, but bigger than many of the dining rooms where Victoria had so often put on displays for dinner entertainments. The guards knelt in front of the audience.

Caenis was shoved back by the slaves and eager spectators. She looked longingly at a nearby side door, but no, too many people were crowded between her and it – and she couldn't desert Victoria in any case. An old friend, seeing her distress, let her perch on his couch. She forced a smile of thanks for his consideration.

At last, Victoria and Cram faced each other. Deep down she felt – she didn't know how she felt. Dim. Not defiant; Cram's treachery had knocked even that out of her. But she had no time for feeling just now, anyway. She expected to die. She never had before, even in the arena, not till now. But she'd not leave this room alive. Too many guards, too many hurts, too angry an emperor, too weary, too sick and shaky and light-headed.

She'd deal with Cram first, though. He had betrayed her. Her, and Caenis, and everything she had worked for. She had known he would, whatever Caenis said, whatever he swore – and he had. So she'd kill him. Whether *he* killed her, or the Germans did it afterwards, she'd see him dead.

Cram had begged a spear instead of his staff. Needle hung in its scabbard at his side.

Victoria had only a short knife, but after her brief rest, as the time for action arrived, now that she could do something, her heart began to lift again. She felt better, more alert. She grinned at her cousin. 'Come along, then, Cram. Mustn't keep your posh pal waiting!'

For once, Cram was silent. He faced her cautiously, letting her stalk round him while he swivelled slowly in the centre. Several times she feinted, close in, to tempt him to thrust at her and draw him off balance, but he just jabbed the spear to fend her off. After a minute's circling, she shrugged and limped away. 'Too scared to put on a good show!' she grumbled, loudly. Please the crowd . . . They were starting to shout, to jeer at Cram. It might push him into being less careful.

One of the senators threw a bread roll. Others joined in, hurling plates and cups, cushions, bones, fruit. She lifted a fig and ate it, her first food since noon, and soft enough for her wobbly teeth and bruised mouth. 'Thanks, kind gentlemen!' she called. They laughed – and as she had invited, Cram took advantage of her apparent inattention to attack. She jerked aside, but found she had no longer quite enough speed and strength to dodge and then dive in and snatch the spear as she had meant to do. She was almost spitted. Bad planning.

How could she get past that spear-point? Play it crafty.

She skidded on a bone. Instead of recovering her footing, Victoria let herself fall, crying out as if with pain. Cram hopped in close to stab down at her; from habit she fended off his spear with her right arm, but it was only wrapped, not armoured, the point ripped up her forearm under the cloth and stabbed deep into her upper arm. Cursing her mistake, she twisted, swiped at his ankles trying to cut his heel tendon, missed, but he withdrew into defence again, allowing her to

162

rise. He was as crafty as she was. Craftier. Think!

Blood flowed down her hand. Luckily, the forearm gash was lengthwise, not across the tendons to cripple her, and she could ignore the pain, but blood was pouring from the slash and the upper stab. Maybe a vein was cut. It would make her hand slip on the knife, and loss of blood would weaken her fairly quickly. She was already weaker than she had expected; her head was pounding and she felt drunk. Concentrate! Control! Think!

Caenis lifted a silver fruit dish and tossed it over the crowd's heads to clatter at Victoria's feet. It was a shallow bowl, two full hand-spans wide, on a short leg. The spectators applauded as Victoria snatched it up as a shield, ignoring the pain of her fingers that stopped her getting a good grip on it. Better than nothing – and . . .

She deflected Cram's spear-point in the dish, and again. Go for it! The third time, she used the concave surface to hold the spear, thrust it high, dropped the dish and knife, grabbed the shaft in both hands and twisted it out of Cram's grip. He staggered back; now she'd get the traitor . . .

She was too near the side. She tripped over a mischievously extended foot and landed hard. The spear was jolted from her blood-slippery half-grip, Cram was snatching for his sword . . . Dodge! Roll! Oh, Bouda! He couldn't chase her fast, thank the gods; she managed to scramble to her feet again and skip away across the open arena.

Manoeuvre him round away from her knife and dish . . .

Reading her mind, Cram kicked them both away, lost under the feet of the jeering, betting crowd. His face was twisted in grim determination. Yes, he would kill her if he could, the Morrigan take him, and now he had two hands to use his sword – her sword, curse Vitellius . . . Keep your mind on the job!

She had lost her weapon and her shield both, and was left with her bare hands. Stupid, stupid to risk everything on a single move! Three bad moves – another would kill her. Could she reach the spear, half under a guard's shield, just in front of the Emperor?

Victoria's aches were easing with the heat in the hall and the exercise. She could move more freely, but hid it, limping more awkwardly than necessary to dodge Cram's lurching attacks. Make him underestimate you . . . He carefully stayed between her and the spear. Without its support, he was very clumsy. But he'd get her eventually, she would slip or trip on the junk scattered round the floor – or he would, which might give her a chance . . .

The junk. Maybe . . .

As if in desperation – and not far wrong – she started snatching up and throwing the smaller articles scattered about the floor, the light or soft ones: cushions, fruit, bones, chunks of bread. Cram fended them off, but they didn't hurt him. After eight or nine had bounced off easily, however hard she

164

threw them, he stopped paying them much attention. Then she threw a heavy goblet. It cracked off his forehead, making him blink and duck – and she was on him like a tiger. Last chance!

She caught his right wrist, his sword hand. He staggered as her weight swung on that arm; his crippled leg couldn't hold them both, and they crashed together on the mosaic floor. Now she had the advantage; she was bigger and stronger, wrestling was a regular part of her training. In seconds she wrenched Needle from him, smashed his mouth with the hilt, and rose to her knees astride him with Needle in her hand. Cram writhed in pain below her.

Shouting, cheering, laughter echoed below the high roof, urging Victoria on. He had betrayed her . . . he would have killed her . . . he hated her. Kill him.

Automatically, as she had been trained, she looked towards the Emperor, master of the games, for his decision.

Vitellius, all the pouches of his face plummy with excitement, was leaning forward, laughing. At Victoria's glance he triumphantly, ceremoniously raised a hand, thumb poised sideways, relishing the power. Then, to the cheers of the massed courtiers, he stabbed the thumb downwards.

Beneath Victoria, Cram stopped wriggling, his face white under smeared blood from the cup's gash across his forehead and her cut arm. He turned his head and spat a tooth on the mosaic. 'So, Boudicca. It finishes. As the gods decide. Rome will still be destroyed.' He frowned. 'What are you waiting for?'

What was she waiting for? She must kill him. She had killed so often at an Emperor's command, it was her duty . . .

Even now? At Vitellius's orders?

And this time her pleasure . . .

Was it?

She hadn't killed Nero.

She could smell Cram's perfume, and his sweat, and his blood.

On her bench near the back, Caenis looked pale and strained.

Suddenly, Victoria shoved herself to her feet. 'No,' she said in Iceni, swaying dizzily. 'I will not. The last man I killed with this sword was the man I loved. My own blood has joined his on her blade. I'll not stain her now with the blood of a traitor!'

'They'll kill you.' Cram sat up gingerly, nursing his jaw.

'They're going to kill me anyway. This sword, my own Needle — your father it was who gave her to me. How can I face his spirit in the Land of Gold if I use her to kill his son?'

Ignoring the roar of puzzled comment and question, Cram spat blood again. 'You always were a fool.' He suddenly grinned bitterly, wincing. 'Remember that time we were driving, and I asked if you wanted to drive to the moon? And you said yes? I loved you for it. And I find I still do, curse you! Surprising, isn't it? And sickening.'

Vitellius was shouting demands to know what Victrix thought she was playing at, what they were saying. Cram flicked one scornful glance at the furious Emperor, and shoved himself to his knees as if for the mercy stroke. 'Fight on, cousin, as the druid commanded you. Drive to the moon, and the Morrigan take you!'

What was he planning? She didn't know.

Yes, she did.

'Go!' He snatched up the spear lying forgotten near their feet and hurled himself across the line of guards, right at the Emperor, bellowing, 'Death! Death to Rome!'

Victoria was already running towards the side door behind Caenis, yelling, 'Come on, Caenis!' Helmann jumped forward, shoving another guard aside in his eagerness to stop her, swinging his huge sword. She ducked, not enough – but he missed, crashing chips off a marble step. Missed? The Germans never missed – not by accident . . . Favour for favour; she managed to turn her wrist and hit him only with the flat of her sword, he staggered as if knocked aside and slipped on some fruit, impeding another guard. She vaulted onto a table, mountaineered over the packed furniture towards the doorway behind, swiped at any senatorial head or hand foolishly raised near her feet.

Snatching up a table knife, Caenis clawed and slashed to join her.

Beyond the couches Victoria jumped down, gasping, and

167

forged a path through the standing spectators, sucking Caenis after her.

No-one tried to halt them. Several of the palace slaves remembered her and Caenis kindly, and either swayed to let them pass unhindered or at least stood still, reluctant to harm them. Some even pretended fear at her sword, flinched aside, pushing slower or more hostile people out of the way, and then stepped back to obstruct the pursuers. Helmann was first among these; apparently accidentally, he tripped as he jumped down from the tables, windmilled his arms and his sword to catch his balance, and so delayed the others yet more, giving Victoria time to tug the door open, yank Caenis out, and slam the door behind them.

A guard had tripped Cram, and as he sprawled across the table his spear-point stabbed down too soon, into the couch cushions just in front of Vitellius's jowls. The guards' long swords pierced him before he could strike a second time.

He gazed up at the ceiling, painted as a glorious sky full of gods, and smiled. 'The Golden Land – beautiful . . .' No-one heard his whisper fade.

Above him, patchy purple-and-grey with rage and fright, spraying spittle, Vitellius was shrieking, 'Get her! Get them! Bring them back! Bring them back alive or dead, or you die, all of you! All of you! Go on, what are you waiting for? Traitors, idiots!'

The guards charged after Caenis and Victoria, heaving

furniture out of their way with no concern for anyone. They had failed in their duty. These conspirators had come near to killing their Emperor. Their pride was hurt – and they would be executed if they failed to find and arrest the escaping pair. They must catch them.

Of course they would catch them.

A wounded cripple and an old woman, stumbling through the labyrinths of the Domus Aurea? Inside a city closed off from the outside, with soldiers almost shoulder to shoulder round the walls? How could they possibly escape?

XII

'What now?' Caenis panted. 'They'll be on us . . .'

Victoria heaved up a solid ivory bench and jammed it sideways behind the big bronze door handles. 'That'll hold them for a minute. Come on, it's just round here, I think – oh, Bouda . . . If I can only remember . . .' She pulled Caenis round a bend in the corridor. 'Ah, found it!'

She twisted the camouflaged handle of a door, curved and painted to vanish into the painted wall-panels. It led into a plain-plastered store-room, and the service passages beyond.

'I didn't know this was here!' Caenis exclaimed.

'Let's hope the guards don't either. I don't know all of them myself.'

As Victoria shut the little door behind them, she heard the clatter of the stool breaking and falling free, and the din of the guards pouring along the corridor – please, Bouda . . .

They ran right past.

Wrapping the tunic as tight as she could round her bleeding arm, she led Caenis through the tangle of cramped tunnels. Their only light came from lamps in the main rooms and corridors, penetrating faintly though tiny windows hidden high in the painted walls. They got good warning of approaching slaves, carrying little lamps as they scurried or dawdled by, and had time to draw aside into cupboards or even, once, out into a guest bedroom where a man lay snoring . . . He did not wake.

Eventually, with a puff of relief, Victoria opened a door out into a normal corridor, lit by small hanging lamps every fifteen paces or so, which led past the offices and kitchens towards the long slave dormitories at the rear of the palace. They hurried silently up a shadowy stair, to a row of small, close-set doors.

'Where are we?' Caenis asked.

'The middling slaves' cubicles, the people just big enough not to be stacked in a dormitory, but not really important. Fortuna forbid she's been moved down again.'

'Who?'

'The only person who might really help us. I think – yes, I think it was this door.' Victoria knocked, and slumped against the wall.

After a long moment, the door opened a crack. Acte's huge eyes peeked out and lit up with joy. 'Victrix – I mean, Victoria! Yes, do come in – no, don't wait out there! Who's that? Oh, Lady Caenis. Er, yes, good, wonderful, er – come in, come in, sit down! Oh, we've been so worried about you!' She hastily closed the door as Caenis helped Victoria in.

A small figure wriggled out from under the bed that filled most of the tiny room.

Needle was poised before Victoria's eyes focused. Then she almost dropped the sword. 'Oppio?'

'Oh, Isis! What are you doing here?' Caenis demanded.

'Couldn't get home from the Circus, could I? City gates is shut tighter'n a duck's arse, an' the bridges too. Guards at the Raudusculum Gate wouldn't let me out, nor them at the Lavernalis; but that Boioric, he telled me you'd come in, lady, so I went up to Lady Caenis's house, thought you'd be there an' Lucius'd find me a bed. But he telled me about you bein' arrested, Lady Caenis, just after the mistress left for the fightin' at the temple, so I went up there an' seen you bein' hauled off, Lady Vic . . . Were that fire, you? Thought so. Wowee! So anyhow, I couldn't think what to do. So I come here to ask Miss Acte what were happenin', an' see could I get you out, an' then you knocked. So we're all here.' Grinning, the boy shrugged. 'What we gonna do, lady?'

Collapsing on Acte's bed beside Caenis, Victoria puffed. 'Let me get my breath back!' Everybody always asked her! But he had come to rescue her; he was a good lad.

Seeing Victoria's wounds clearly in the light of Acte's little lamp, Caenis was horrified. 'That's first, anyway. You should have said, Victoria! I didn't realise . . . Acte, have you a cloth I can use for a bandage? No, don't tear up your good dress – oh, you shouldn't have! But thank you, dear, yes, nice soft linen, it's perfect.'

While Caenis competently bound up the arm, Acte passed

172

round her cup of watered wine. Victoria drank thirstily, but her head spun as wildly as before.

'We must get out right away,' Caenis declared firmly, tying the last knot. 'Acte, everybody knows you're Victoria's friend. Your room will be searched as soon as they think of it. We've brought you danger, asking you to risk helping us.'

'I'm sorry, Acte, but you were my only hope,' Victoria apologised.

'Oh, no, anything I can do . . . You're my friend, Vicky. My true friend.' Acte looked vaguely round. 'Since – since Nero died, life isn't the same.'

She had no more expressive words to describe her forlorn loneliness. No longer an emperor's favourite, she had lost all the status she had scarcely noticed that she had. Most of her friends had dropped away as soon as they could get no more from her. Almost everything Nero had given her had been either officially removed, or 'borrowed' permanently by slaves who had envied her former privileges, and she had been moved to this poky, out-of-the-way room. Two plain gowns hung on a rope in one corner, above a single wooden stool. Her bed was narrow and hard, and though the cover was embroidered it was worn and faded.

Victoria gathered her thoughts. 'Is there a terrace outside?'

'Er – no, Vicky. Just the roof of a dormitory.'

'Just as good, Acte, we can jump down from there, and the window here's large enough to climb out.'

Caenis blinked. 'I can't squeeze out of windows and jump off roofs, not at my age!'

'You'd rather stay and be executed? Along with Acte?' Victoria demanded.

'Hmm. Since you put it like that, no, I suppose not. But you'll have to help me.'

Acte was surprised. 'Jump off the roof? Why? Why not just walk down the stair at the end of the corridor, to the garden door?' She shrugged, puzzled but accommodating. 'If you *want* to climb out, of course—'

'No, no, Acte, the stairs sound perfect,' Caenis protested. 'Windows and roofs indeed! How silly can you get? Don't answer that, dear, I was talking to Victoria, not you!' Victoria felt too weak to smile. 'Everybody's in bed — everybody sensible, that is. Excellent thinking, dear.'

Acte blushed, unused to such compliments.

'I knows where we c'n climb the palace wall easy,' Oppio put in. 'Even you, Lady Caenis!'

'Such a nuisance being old and infirm!' Caenis was snippy.

'Yeah, but I'll help you over, lady,' he chirped.

'Thank you, son.' She grimaced, ruefully. 'With you and your mistress around I'll never get vain.'

Victoria paid no attention. She was woozily surprised and pleased; Acte having a good idea! A good omen for the rest of the night. She hauled herself to her feet and kissed her friend. 'Thank you, Acte. May all the gods bless you, dear! I'll make a sacrifice on your behalf as soon as we're free.'

'And on your cousin's, too, Victoria.' Caenis's voice was sombre. 'He must be dead.'

'I suppose so. Yes.' Victoria's heart felt clenched. He had hated her, and loved her and died for her . . . She drew a long breath. 'But that's for later. Got to get moving now. Oppio, check the corridor is empty, and we'll be on our way. Oh – have you a wrap I can borrow, Acte?'

'We'll take away that stained tunic, dear, and pour away the bloody water in the garden, not to leave any trace of us.' Caenis was always practical.

'Hey, Miss Acte, why not come with us? Safer, I'll bet.'

Acte was startled and dismayed at Oppio's suggestion. 'Leave? No, I couldn't! No, this is my home. I couldn't!' However dreary her life nowadays, the palace still held her memories of Nero. She'd not be persuaded. She led them down the empty stair, kissed them farewell, and bolted the door behind them to hide their exit.

They never knew that just two minutes later a dozen Germans were battering at Acte's door, barking questions in faulty Latin. 'Trail of blood to here – bloody handmarks by your door! Where they go? Where they go?' Confused and petrified by their shouts and blows, unable to answer so many at once, Acte was still smiling appeasingly as they killed her.

★ ★ ★

For twenty minutes, Oppio led Caenis and Victoria creeping through the grounds of the Domus Aurea. Once they lay flat behind a rose-bed as a dozen soldiers ran past, blinded by the light of their own torches. Another time, as the fugitives flitted among sculptured shrubberies they disturbed some gazelles which bounded huffily off; Caenis nearly gave them away by yelping, and again when an unnoticed patrol charged after the pattering of the hoofs. Then in an elegant copse a searching guard actually tripped over Victoria's ankle, but she lay so still that he thought she was simply a root and hurried on.

When they finally reached a distant corner where a branch overhung the wall, there was no-one about. Caenis graciously and gratefully accepted Oppio's hand to help her climb up and crawl along to drop to the street beyond. Victoria managed – just – to clamber over unaided.

Caenis looked round to get her bearings as soon as they were out of view from the palace wall. 'This way. I know a silversmith who will take us in.'

'No, Caenis.' There was nothing Victoria wanted more than to lie down, but only if it was safe. 'I'm hard to hide. I've got to get right out. I'm the one Vitellius wants specially. You and Domitian as well, of course—'

'Don't worry about Domitian,' Caenis said firmly. 'That young man always finds a way to evade trouble. Once you got him out of the temple he'll have found some school friend

176

who'll help him. And I'll be safe enough, I'm very ordinary-looking—'

'You ain't!' Oppio protested.

She chuckled. 'A compliment at last! No, son, three maids work hard to keep me looking respectable. I'm not terribly important, though. Not to Vitellius. But you, Victoria – you've publicly hurt his pride. I think you're right, you should leave the city. If you can.'

'I'll manage.' Victoria felt a feather would knock her down, but there was no point in worrying Caenis. 'You go on. Oppio, see her safe, and then go to the Blues' stables, you'll be safe there. Can you do that?'

'No problem, lady!' Proud as any legionary standard-bearer, Oppio drew his knife and puffed out his puny chest. 'I'll look arter you, Lady Caenis! Don't you fret about nowt!'

Caenis's teeth shone as she smiled briefly. 'You're a hero, Oppio! Will you check that street there? I'll join you in a moment.' He trotted off, while Caenis hugged Victoria. 'The next few days will be dreadful, my dear. Primus will attack. There will be fighting in the streets. You must, you must get out – but be careful!'

'When am I not?' Victoria asked, and was surprised when Caenis huffed a shaky laugh at her. 'Sure you want to stay, Caenis? If it's so bad, will you be safe in Rome?'

'Safer than I'd be trying to escape past all these soldiers hunting for us. You can climb walls, Victoria, which is a touch beyond me. Besides, I have to do what I can for my servants. Fortuna and all your own gods watch over you!' Caenis kissed her and slipped away after Oppio.

Once alone, Victoria sagged. Climb walls? She doubted if she could walk without leaning on walls for support.

By the time she found the yard and her ponies, she couldn't.

The smoke from the burning temple had made Lightning and Thunder uneasy and fretful. Victoria talked quietly to them, rubbed their noses and necks, reassured them. They had a tub of water and a bucket of oats; she chewed a couple of handfuls, like raw porridge. Drinking plain water was dangerous, as everyone knew, but she was so thirsty that she gulped it gratefully. Then she sat down and tried to gather her strength. Slowly, slowly . . .

As she decided she was, she must be, recovered enough to drive, Oppio arrived. She sighed. 'Oh, Bouda! You never do what you're told. Should have known . . . But I'm glad to see you.'

He grinned. 'Somebody gotta look arter you, lady!'

'Caenis is safe? Good. Harness them for me, son, this finger's murdering me. Are any of the city gates still open? Maybe down south?'

'Neh, shouldn't think so.' Oppio shook his shaggy head as he opened the yard gate and hopped up to kneel behind her. 'Seems t' me, wi' some o' your pals bein' at the Lavernalis, best try there. If you asks nice they could let you drop over while their officer ain't lookin', an' walk home if they ain't heard about you pissin' on the Emperor. Or the chariot's light, they might even lift it over for you, an' the horses could jump down if they ain't built the wall up too high.'

It seemed the best bet.

Victoria drove east and then south, right round the Circus Maximus, staying as far away as she could from the palace and possible search parties. The people scurrying about in the dark, wet streets, lit only by a few lanterns hung out as the law required, were furtively busy about their own affairs.

Oppio had been right; as they passed the Porta Raudusculana, the other way out to the Ostia road, sentries and soldiers were blocking the closed gates with stone and timber against attack by a battering ram – or by the hysterical crowd trying to get out.

Round the Aventine Hill to her usual Porta Lavernalis, where she drew up before entering the open space in front of the gateway. Another crowd was surging about, waving fists and cudgels and even a few swords, shouting, weeping, only held back from charging the barricade by a bad-tempered line of the German soldiers who were building it.

Oppio sucked his teeth, a habit copied from his hero Balbus. 'Won't let nobody out, not wi' all them lot there, not even you, lady,' he observed dolefully. 'What we gonna do now?'

'Oh, Bouda! How should I know? Go and hold the ponies' heads while I think.' Shivering, and not just with cold, Victoria sat back on her heels on the floor of the little chariot, and tried to focus her woozy thoughts.

Fifty paces away, the barricade now ran right across the gateway, a solid dam of wood and stone as high as her head. The German guards had made a ramp of one of the huge old gates and a sullen work party was rolling barrels from a nearby warehouse up it, to build a protective wall along the outer edge of the barrier. 'Three deep on the bottom an' two on top! No, tight up, you dozy savages!' their centurion was shouting hoarsely. Though a ballista would break the barricade, it would be hard to bring one up among the warehouses, and the curtain wall was high and strong enough to keep out javelins and infantry as long as the attackers didn't grab the barrels with grapnels and pull them out and down.

The guards were preparing for that, though; the centurion was driving them to nail heavy baulks of timber and iron chains to hold them firm: 'No, not there, across the top! Never seen a hammer before? Never done a day's work in your lazy lives! Oh, for a decent legion! Half a dozen trained men even! Mithras gimme patience before I knock your thick Gerry skulls into meatballs an' fry 'em for supper!'

As she watched, a guard carrying one end of a beam up the ramp stumbled on the top edge of the wooden gate, which jutted a hand's breadth above the main barrier walkway. Off-balanced by his burden, he fell hard against the curtain wall. Three of the upper barrels fell off outside, and as the man tried

180

to stop them toppling he knocked down two more.

The centurion welted the soldier with his ash stick. 'One-legged dimwit! Go an' get me another dozen barrels! Yes, you, you stinkin' cowpat, you an' your hairy mates!'

The heckling mob agreed with him. 'Cack-handed Gerries, can't even build a wall! Think that's gonna keep Primus out, eh?'

It was the last straw. The centurion might insult his soldiers, but nobody else could! 'Clear these scumbags off, lads, give us room to breathe! Move 'em!'

Delighted at taking action at last against their tormentors – and escaping temporarily from the tiring, undignified labouring – the Germans flashed out their long swords. The crowd squealed and fled before them, up past Victoria or sideways along the roads just inside the wall. Oppio struggled to hold the ponies steady as the German soldiers charged past, a couple recognising her and waving as they went by.

Suddenly, Oppio let go the reins and appeared at Victoria's knee, whispering eagerly, 'Over the top? Lady? Look, lady, there's a gap now, right at the top o' that ramp, an' the crowd's out o' the way.'

'Oppio, that's crazy!'

'No it ain't!' He swung up behind her, leaning forward to hiss in her ear. 'Yer chariot's strong, you built it y'self, lady, told me it'd go up a mountain, anywheres. Go on, we can do it! Go on!'

Victoria was tempted. Her head felt light enough to float right over anything and carry the chariot with her . . . It was hard to think straight. 'The horses would end up hanging on the far side and us stuck back here like a seesaw. And no wheels could take a drop that high, we'd smash.' She must be crazy too, to even consider it. Unwarily she shook her head and had to grab it to stop it falling off.

The first new barrels reached the top of the ramp and thumped off the upper end, to lie on their sides against the outer wall. The Germans shoving them stopped.

'Put 'em up?' – Their voices came faintly over the shouting behind Victoria.

'Na, he'll say they in wrong place' – 'I know where I want to put them!' – 'Ya, up his fat bum, one after other, eh? But better we wait till he come back.'

Huffily, they sat down to rest.

'Go on, lady!' Oppio urged. 'Them barrels on their sides makes a step up now, see, all rounded, an' Lightnin' an' Thunder's light on their feet, they'll not fall.'

'No!' Oh, why did he keep arguing? 'They'd break their legs.'

'Worth it if we got away! You c'n always get new horses! In the Circus they goes through horses like a mule eatin' radishes; it don't matter, you gotta gamble to win!'

Victoria puffed, surprised at her reluctance to risk the stupid animals. Her Iceni training must have had more effect than she realised. Or was it just another softness? No, it was sensible. 'Too risky. Not a gamble, a certainty, they'd just have to pick up the bits outside. No, don't go on about it. Not unless we have to. And we don't.'

Behind her someone shouted, 'There she is! See her against the bonfires!' A triumphant yell arose. A squad of guards was charging towards her.

Oppio gasped in terror.

That settled it. Now they had to.

She spread her knees wide, yelled, 'Hang on tight for your life! Go, Thunder, go, Lightning, go, go!' She drew Needle and stabbed her ponies' rumps.

Screaming, they bolted forward, whisking the chariot across the open square. Soldiers and stragglers leapt for their lives. She stuck Needle into a side spar of the chariot – no need to lose her sword again so soon . . . never mind that, concentrate! – and held the ponies straight with the last of her strength, onto the short, steep ramp, hooves thundering up the heavy wood, jolting the chariot up after them. The soldiers at the top jumped straight down off the barricade. 'Bounce!' she yelled to Oppio, and did so herself, to make the light vehicle jounce up off the ramp's tip instead of dropping into the hollow behind it. 'Go, go!' Panicking, hurt, trusting her voice, the ponies sprang onto and then out over the barrels into the blackness beyond. The little chariot's wheels, bounding high, crashed and rolled on the rounded horizontal barrels, tossed the chariot high to clear the standing barrels beyond and soar after the ponies into the darkness.

A moment of terrifying, thrilling suspense, flying, flying . . . Drive to the moon . . .

'Woweeeee!' Oppio screeched in delighted terror.

Crash down.

Thunder stumbled, was thrust up by Lightning's shoulder before he could fall; they lunged frantically forward, bolted down the road. Behind them the light, supple chariot bounced high, and again, and again, and then rolled on and away.

Victoria's knee burst through the leather floor, which helped hold her down. But no broken wheels, no broken pole, no broken axle. No broken arms or legs or necks.

Oppio didn't appreciate the sheer luck that had saved them. Full of the thrill of their escape, of the bouncing that had tossed him flying, held down only by his fists gripping the side arches, he swivelled round to shrill gleefully back, 'Bye-bye, mugs!'

At last the ponies slowed themselves to a canter, a jolting trot, a gasping, limping, unhappy halt. Oppio jumped down and ran forward to their heads, to grab the reins close to the bits, talking soothingly, still laughing. 'Hush now. You're all right, Thunder. It's all over. Calm down, Lightnin'. Hush now, settle down! Oh, Lady Vic, you should be the Blues' driver, not me! Never seen nowt like that, never! Wait till I tells the lads! Got a spoke broke there – lucky it ain't worse, eh? That leg hurts, Thunder? Quiet, good lad. Calm, eh. That's better. Hush now, hush. Need to get a move on, though, lady, them as dropped over the wall'll be after us. Thunder's strained a hock but he'll make it home.'

He got no answer.

'Lady? Lady Vic!'

She was collapsed, unconscious. The bandage on her arm was soggy with blood. Maybe dying?

And heavy army boots were clattering on the cobbles not far behind.

XIII

'Oh, I wish I'd seen it all!' Almost a year later, Julia Felix lay back in her long chair on Caenis's terrace, laughing delightedly.

'So do I!' Chuckling, Victoria sipped her hot spiced wine. 'I don't remember a thing after charging the wall. Oppio was the hero of the night. The guards found horses somewhere and galloped after us. Luckily, my horses knew the way home, while Oppio hung onto me to stop me falling out, and yelled so loud the porter opened up in time to let him drive right in. Between them they managed to slam the gates right in the faces of the guards. The noise roused the household, of course. So Smarandax pretended he was still half asleep and argued with the centurion through the grille in the gate, and then Oppio did his innocent, scared little boy act. "Yessir, Lady Vic drove over the barrier, yessir, but when the horses stopped down the road she dropped off, told me to drive fast 'ome, sir, an' get in an' not open up, see! I just done what she said, sir. She said as she'd hide among the river warehouses. That's the last I seen 'er, sir, honest!" '

'Honest he'll never be, that little rascal. But didn't they demand to get in to search?' the old lady asked.

'Oh, of course, but Africa chased them off. She had all the

186

girls up on the wall by this time, waving weapons, cursing and shouting challenges, while she yelled, "You calling us liars, you stinking dog-breath? Who d'you think you're dealing with – sleazy floozies behind the Circus Maximus? We're the Amazons, an' you'll set foot inside over my dead body – an' yours!" '

Caenis was chuckling. 'I'd back those girls of yours against a full cohort any day, never mind a handful of German auxiliaries!'

'So what happened? Tell me, girl! Your version is far more exciting than Caenis's letters!'

'Well, what d'you think happened? I'm here to tell you about it!' Victoria shrugged. 'Their centurion blustered a bit and then they slouched off with their faces tripping them. And that was that. I just wish I'd been awake – Mira bandaged me up again, but I was barely conscious for days. Oppio boasts to his pals in the Blues that he beat five troops of cavalry in the race to the house, and faced down a general all on his own.'

'The Amazons were ready to fight to defend you?' Julia Felix asked. 'Amazing!'

'Yes, every single one – quite a compliment, eh?' Caenis raised her goblet to Victoria.

'Even against their German friends. I don't understand it,' Victoria said. 'Not that I'm unhappy about it, but I don't know why.'

'It's not difficult to understand, plum.' Caenis smiled gently. 'You'd looked after and fought for them, they said, so they'd look after and fight for you. Though they put it much less politely!'

Victoria, to her astonishment, found herself blushing, and hid her face in her wine cup.

'What happened to them?' Julia Felix asked.

'The Germans or the Amazons?' Caenis asked mischievously, making the old lady tut and wag an exasperated finger at her.

'We never saw any of the Germans again,' Victoria told her, regretfully. 'When Primus attacked Rome two days later they fought for Vitellius like lions. And died.'

Caenis nodded, her face grim. 'Primus's men had to take the city street by street, with people watching from their windows and balconies, eating picnics and cheering on the fighters as if it was a set of games. That didn't help the soldiers' temper any.'

As Caenis stopped, unwilling to go on, Victoria finished the tale. 'Primus found Vitellius deserted and alone in the Domus Aurea, dragged him out to the Forum, killed him and threw his body on the Capitoline Steps, just like Sabinus. I'm told the crowd kicked and spat on it, the same as on Sabinus's body just three days before. But then Primus and his men went on a rampage through Rome, like Cremona. The silversmith who had taken Caenis in – his house was attacked and everybody there killed.'

'What?' Julia Felix stared. 'You never told me this, Caenis! How did you escape?'

'I wasn't there,' Caenis said briefly.

'No. I'd lost so much blood, they thought I was dying, and Oppio dared creep into Rome past the fighting, to beg Caenis to come and nurse me,' Victoria explained. 'He slipped her away just before the sack began. She probably saved my life, Fortuna bless her, but that maybe saved hers.'

Caenis sighed. Julia Felix patted her hand in sympathy. 'Yes, mourn them, my dear. But if you'd been killed by his own men, Vespasian would have been devastated.' As Caenis only sighed again, Julia Felix shook her head. 'Sacking Rome! Terrible! Perhaps Jupiter was avenging the sacrilege of breaking sanctuary in his temple and then burning it.'

'Maybe.' Victoria nodded. She had certainly been hurt after doing that; maybe it was indeed a punishment. 'I was on my feet again by the time Governor Mucianus arrived from Syria as Vespasian's official representative. He executed lots more senators.' Not that she mourned any of them.

'And Vitellius's seven-year-old son.' Caenis looked bleak.

'He and Primus saved Vespasian a lot of future trouble, girl!' Julia Felix snapped. 'Don't be soft! Vespasian didn't complain, did he?'

'When they'd gained Rome for him? Scarcely. Though he was furious with Primus, in private.' Caenis straightened her shoulders. 'Yes, I know, it had to be done. And things will improve now . . . I just wish it hadn't cost so much – so many people dead!'

'Politics.' Victoria sighed too, but shook herself out of despondency. 'Caenis, everybody dies some time. But we've finally succeeded.'

For now, at last, Vespasian had arrived in Rome. His coronation procession was parading round the city so that the crowds could see him – through the streets, round the Circus Maximus, and then across the Forum up to the hastily repaired Temple of Jupiter on the Capitol, where he would don the imperial gold laurel wreath and make his first sacrifice as Emperor and High Priest of Rome.

From Caenis's terrace, the three women could look between roofs and see a short stretch of the route, fifty paces away. 'You didn't want to be nearer, get a better view, Caenis?' Victoria asked. 'You could have hired a window right on the road.'

Caenis shook her head. 'I've seen enough processions.'

Julia Felix chuckled. 'What a year – the Year of the Four Emperors! Galba, Otho, Vitellius, and now Vespasian.'

Smiling, Caenis sipped her wine. 'I can't go up to the Capitol with him, to see him crowned. I can see all I need to from up here, in comfort, without the stink of sweat and the deafening trumpets and drums and shouting, and the dust while the legions and carts file past, and all the razzamatazz. I know he's there, and he knows I'm here. That's enough. Besides, do you know how much hiring a room down there costs? Vespasian says we have to watch the expenses!'

They all laughed; Rome could have afforded the cost of a

190

window for the mistress of the Emperor – or he could have simply taken it, if he had been that kind of man. But he wasn't; that was why they had supported him. Caenis smirked, affectionately teasing: 'Besides, it would be too tiring for Julia Felix. We have to take care of feeble old ladies!'

'Feeble? Stick your ear over here, girl, and I'll show you who's feeble!' her friend snapped, pretending annoyance.

'Sorry, sorry! You're tougher than both of us put together!' Caenis apologised. 'But I'm chilly. October is cool – good for the parade, of course, the soldiers won't be boiled in their armour, but sitting watching is less pleasant. Lucius! I'm going to get a shawl. Julia?'

Julia Felix nodded reluctantly at the tactful offer. 'Feeble old lady, eh? Oh, very well, very well, girl! And some more hot wine.'

'Lucius, bring out the warmed blankets and socks. Yes, all right, Julia, I admit I had them ready, don't go huffy! Victoria, give us all a refill, will you, please?' Caenis asked.

As Victoria lifted the jug from its bronze tripod above the little brazier between her and Julia Felix, her arm twinged and jerked, and she spilt some on the red tiles. 'Oh, I'm sorry, Caenis—'

'No, no!' Caenis smiled away the apology while she tucked a soft woolly shawl round Julia Felix's bony shoulders. 'An extra gift to the gods – a sign of good fortune, dear. Lucius, pour for us, please. How is your arm now, Victoria?'

Stretching, Victoria regarded it sourly. 'Not wonderful. I can use it, but as you see it jerks uncontrollably sometimes. Manny says a tendon is permanently damaged, it will probably never be strong and steady enough for the arena. So I may never fight again.' She tried to hide the bitterness and frustration of that. But she'd not give in. Never. She'd prove Manny wrong – Bouda help her, she would!

Caenis nodded. 'Good. Yes, good, my dear! You've taken more than enough wounds.'

Victoria blinked. That was a new thought. Maybe . . .? 'No, it's not that. I admit' – with some surprise – 'when I think about a combat I don't feel that special tingle of excitement and fear, my heart doesn't leap at the thought any more . . . But I'm not afraid of fighting!'

Caenis tutted reproof. 'You? Afraid? Don't be silly!'

Victoria had to laugh. How terrified she had felt, often, before every fight, or facing Vitellius – and now at the thought of never fighting again! 'Maybe I'm getting old.'

'Old? You're not twenty yet!' Julia Felix huffed. 'Still your mother's milk wet on your lips! When you're half my age you can start talking about being old!'

'So what will you do now?' Caenis asked, gently. 'You're not the type just to live on your money, be a lady of leisure!'

'Oh, how boring!' Victoria grimaced, and smiled at her friend's concerned face. It was hard to hide her frustration – but why worry her friends? 'Don't fret about me, Caenis. I'll go on as a lanista.'

'You can't kill, so you'll train killers?' Julia Felix sounded intrigued, not disapproving.

'Fighters.' Victoria was vexed. Everybody thought that it was the killing that was important, not the combat! 'No, I can't fight personally. I suppose I'll get used to the idea.' Though not if she could help it; the old glories would return! 'But there will always be games and gladiators. People will always fight. I can help my girls stay alive, fight well, win fame and fortune. And take a commission for it. Why not?'

She made herself grin cheerfully. 'Africa will stay with us, she's happy to let me be boss and have the bother of organising the Amazons, but she'll be our star fighter for now, though we've got several promising new girls. And she's a great trainer. And little Celia – she's lightning with an abacus, so she's going to learn to keep our accounts. I'll have the finest palaestra in the Empire.'

'And a family.' Julia Felix nodded at her. 'That's important to you, isn't it?'

Yes, she'd have a family again. Smarandax, and Mira, and Celia, and that little rascal Oppio. Not her own family, maybe, but near enough – someone to care for, to care for her . . . The thought, as always, cheered Victoria's heart like sunshine on a cold winter day.

Slowly, Caenis nodded. 'I wish you the very best of good fortune.' Good wishes this time were not unlucky. Victoria suddenly felt such a bubbling happiness, she almost missed her friend's next words. 'But how can we — how can Vespasian reward you for all you've done?'

What was that? Reward? Ah. Wake up, Victoria, pay attention!

'After all, dear, you've risked your life for him. Without you he'd likely not be emperor. You've saved his son's life, and mine. By the way, did Domitian ever actually thank you? No? Stupid, rude boy . . . Vespasian owes you an enormous debt. So . . . Your Villa Glauca is a wreck, dear. I wondered if you would like this house.'

'Live among all the snooty snobs here when you move to the palace with Vespasian? Yeugh!' Victoria didn't trouble to hide a shudder, and pursed her lips thoughtfully as they laughed. 'Thanks, but I'll stay out at the palaestra. But I have been considering this, very carefully.' She puffed, not quite sure how to go on.

Julia Felix chuckled drily. 'Watch out, Caenis, this sounds expensive!'

'Well, yes,' Victoria admitted. 'But useful too. I think so, anyway.'

She gestured across the houses before them, over the artificial lake towards the gleaming sprawl of the Domus Aurea. 'You said Vespasian said Cosy Corner there was a ridiculous waste of money and space, and he was trying to think how to use it better.'

'Ye-es?' Caenis looked intrigued — and wary.

194

'Every emperor builds something to be remembered by, temples or roads or aqueducts or palaces. Well . . .' Go for it, girl! Victoria drew a deep breath. 'There isn't a decent arena in Rome. Not since the great fire. The Circus Maximus was rebuilt, but no arenas.'

'Now there's a thought,' Julia Felix observed. 'Augustus built temples, Claudius built the new harbour at Ostia. Why shouldn't Vespasian build an arena?'

'It could go right where that overgrown puddle is. It'd be popular, that's certain, among the people and the Senate.' Victoria's argument was valid; Caenis nodded. 'If you really want to reward me, build me a place where I can work. Even if I can't fight, I can still produce great fighters. Give me – give Rome – a great place to see them!'

'The Flavian Amphitheatre.' Caenis was thoughtful. 'The biggest and best in the world. That sounds like an excellent idea. And so suitable, to thank a gladiatrix! I think Vespasian would like it. Yes, I really do. I can't guarantee it, but . . . You'd help plan it, Victoria? You've been all round the world, you've seen the best arenas from the inside, you can tell the architects and builders what to put in and how best to arrange it.'

'Rooms and cages underneath for the scenery and fighters and beasts, and trapdoors over lifts and ramps to bring them up fast and surprise the crowd.' Victoria's voice was eager. 'And the aqueducts that feed the lake now could provide water for naval battles—'

195

'Got it all worked out, girl, eh?' Julia Felix raised her glass. 'Here's to your success, Victoria Victrix, the finest gladiatrix ever!'

'Thank you – and to the Flavian Amphitheatre! May it be the finest arena ever, and put on the finest games!' said Victoria.

'And to Vespasian, who will build it. Let him be the finest emperor ever, and realise all our hopes!' Caenis added.

Victoria smiled as they drank. Boudicca's command was fulfilled; she had destroyed the worst part of Rome, the part that had destroyed Britain. Boudicca, and her aunt and uncle, and the father she had never known, and even Cram, would welcome her to the Golden Land.

Below them, on the Via Sacra, two black horses drew into view a golden chariot bearing a burly man in a general's uniform, with an imperial purple cloak. 'Look! There he is now!' Victoria cried. Even at that distance she could make out Vespasian's jutting jaw and eyebrows, and the lines of determination and humour in his face.

They all jumped up together: the society lady, the freedwoman, and the gladiatrix. Julia Felix was chuckling in triumphant delight, clutching a slipping shawl. Caenis was trembling, hands clasped, biting her lip, smiling, sudden helpless tears running unchecked down her cheeks. Victoria drew Needle, whistled shrilly though her fingers, and waved her sword vigorously for all of them to cheer on the Emperor they had made.

Glossary

Roman/Latin words are shown [L]
Celtic words are marked [C]

Aeneid [L]	play and long poem about Aeneas, a prince who escaped the fall of Troy; the founder of Rome, according to one legend
Ahura Mazda	Zoroastrian god of light
Apollo [L]	Roman god of the sun, of music and art
as [L]	copper coin (4 asses = 1 sesterce; a small loaf cost 1 as)
atrium [L]	small open-roofed courtyard in Roman house, usually with a central pool
ballista [L]	siege machine for throwing heavy stones
basilica [L]	open-sided hall, its roof supported by columns, used for markets, courts, etc
Bouda [C]	Celtic goddess of victory
Boudicca [C]	British queen (See Book One: *Victoria – Born to Be a Warrior*)
Campus Martius [L]	old army parade grounds just outside the walls of Rome

Capitol [L]
high, steep hill in Rome, site of the original city fortress

Castor and Pollux [L] twin Roman demi-gods, horsemen

Charon
ferryman who carried souls of the dead across the River Styx to the underworld

Circus Maximus [L]
enormous racetrack in Rome for horses and chariots

client
person supporting a patron, e.g. voting for him in the law courts or elections, in return for favours

decurion [L]
under-officer, especially in the cavalry, commanding about 10 soldiers

Domus Aurea [L]
(Golden House) the huge palace built by Nero after fire destroyed half of Rome (see Book Two: *Victrix – Triumph in the Roman Arena*)

editor [L]
organiser of gladiatorial combats, hunts, etc, in Roman arena

equites [L]
(pronounced *eh-quit-ays* meaning horsemen, knights) middle classes, businessmen, the rank below senators; rich enough to equip themselves as fully-armed heavy cavalry; by this time they only wore their armour for ceremonial parades.

Flavian
arena build by Emperor Flavius

Amphitheatre [L]	Vespasianus and his son, Titus. The huge statue of Nero, the Colossus (altered to be a statue of Hercules), was later moved down beside the arena, which then became known as the Colosseum.
Fortuna [L]	Roman goddess of luck
glauca [L]	grey
Hispania [L]	Spain
Judaea [L]	Roman province, modern Israel/Palestine/Lebanon area
Jupiter Optimus Maximus [L]	Jupiter the Best and Greatest, Roman king of the gods
lanista [L]	trainer of gladiators
lictors [L]	ceremonial guards of a magistrate.
Lusitania [L]	Portugal
Mare Nostra [L]	(Our Sea) the Mediterranean
Mithras	Middle Eastern god of light, born in a stable at midwinter, given gifts by shepherds and kings; popular among Roman soldiers.
Moesia [L]	Roman province, approximately Romania
Morrigan, the [C]	British goddess of destruction
Ostia [L]	Rome's port, 20 kilometres from the city at the mouth of the Tiber River
palaestra [L]	training yard of gladiatorial school; the school itself

Praetorian Guard [L]   elite regiment, the Emperor's traditional bodyguard

Praetorian Prefect [L]   Commander of the Praetorian Guard

primus pilus [L]   (first spear) senior centurion of first century of first cohort of a legion; regimental sergeant–major; usually the most experienced soldier of the legion

proconsul [L]   official representative or envoy of Rome; always a former consul

retiarius [L]   light-armoured gladiator with net and trident

Rhiannon [C]   Celtic goddess of music

Romulus [L]   with his brother Remus, original founder and first king of Rome

secutor [L]   heavy-armed gladiator

sesterce [L]   silver coin; a slave cost from 20 sesterces up. You were officially poor if you couldn't afford a slave.

Styx   river across the road to the underworld of the dead

Thracian   light-armed gladiator with small shield and curved sword

tribune [L]   junior officer in army or government

Venus [L]   Roman goddess of love

Vestal Virgins [L]   six priestesses of Vesta, goddess of the hearth, Rome's most revered goddess

vigiles [L]   policemen/firefighters in Rome